I0533164

Escape from Europa

By A. V. Guzzo

ISBN; 978-0-96436-926-9

Cover Artist
Phil Guzzo
studiomongo.com

Escape from Europa

Katherine DeLumiere, Kitty, thought she had it all…until her life fell apart. She was convicted of fomenting revolution and sent up to the Lunar rehabilitation center to determine what treatment would turn her into a "normal" citizen.

But fate had other plans for her that involved the Ice World of Europa and an alter ego that followed her giving her advice she really didn't want.

Dramatis Personae

Time: Terran year 2467

Kitty: A Terran, accused of gun running in the Eritrean revolution.

Iain Cabot. Computer Physicist/engineer sent by Earth's Consortium

Ella: Fellow prisoner on the moon.

Orlando: Leader of the   Eritrean Revolution… betrayed Kitty.

Jason: A guard, who rebelled against his Moon assignment.

Mondara: A planet about one hundred light years from Earth.

  Carg: A Mondaran woman who can appear in Kitty's visual Cortex and can communicate with her in real time.

Brace Adams: Captain of the Escadril.

Laura Adams: Captain Adams wife, lost in a ship wreck five years earlier

Cody Williams: Communications Engineer on the Escadril

Sadoka Engstrom: Chief Engineer on the Escadril **Lex**: Mechanical Engineer on the Escadril

Andrew McNeil: Commander of Lunar Fighter sent to check out the Escadril for stowaways

  John Champion: Friend of Captain Adams, sent to investigate Trawler attack on Europa

Mira: Pleasure Pal on Escadril

Darylin workers in Madam Canzioni's Pleasure Palace on Europa

Escape from Europa

Chapter One

She knew that for centuries the Moon was a symbol of romance and mystery, but it was hardly that now, standing on it, its weak gravity somehow holding you upright, it was instead depressing. Katherine, better known as Kitty DeLumiere, to her friends, was here on business but not the kind that would provide her with comfortable surroundings. Instead she was here as a prisoner having been found guilty of fomenting violence in the Eritrean revolution. But having been found guilty doesn't mean she was guilty. In fact she was innocent.

She was not quite as dark as the other Eritrean women, something about her grandfather had an affair with a European soldier, but her dark eyes made her attractive to Orlando, the Rat.

Now, many years after those emotional centuries which produced people with the moon induced 'wobblies' or those that claimed a more ferocious transformation, the moon was simply an economic necessity. For a variety of reasons, financial being foremost, the Consortium of Terran Nations decided that deportation of convicted felons to the lunar colony was a sensible alternative to an ever expanding, expensive and unworkable prison system on earth. Undeveloped land was rare and costly, considering that the Consortium leaders confiscated vast estates for their own use. While economy was uppermost in leaders minds, there were other priorities. Moon based facilities allowed administrators great freedom in choosing luxurious offices, living quarters and amenities which were well out of sight of Terran authorities. When Terran leaders did visit they approved and shared in the services and luxuries.

This kind of government work attracted many Terrans at least those, unlike Kitty, who were not sentenced to long prison sentences Rather, she was one of the prisoners, labeled as such by her fluorescent green outfit which didn't match her dark hair and against her light brown skin, and just succeeded in making her look ghostly. She was not ghostly, however, according to Orlando, Orlando the Rat, her lover of many years she was exceptionally attractive.

It became the norm to relocate violent felons to other far flung worlds besides Luna where extensive prisons were set up. Moon Base 4, Earth's main prisoner relocation center was the first stop and here the Warden and guards set about efficiently sorting and shipping prisoners to the various prison facilities throughout the developed planets of the solar system, or for a few individuals, treating them medically at the Lunar hospital. Some, after these treatments, were allowed to return to earth as "reformed" individuals.

While some relocation sites had a more Spartan atmosphere, the design engineers were thoughtful enough to provide, at least in Kitty's area, hard plastic backed chairs that fit no one's anatomy, a water cooler and portholes overlooking the pockmarked landscape, a paler version of the Sahara desert Katherine DeLumiere had seen years back on earth in the Eritrean wilderness. In its starkness, the view of the pitted, barren, bleached and radiated landscape was forbidding yet beautiful in its own way, but for someone used to the lushness of earth, this was a difficult transition. Her home, the Eritrean Desert, had life that didn't exist on this landscape.

From the perspective of the Terran Justice system, her case was clear and her punishment appropriate. She had been found by North Consortium government troops guarding stockpiles of weapons and electro shock grenades, all of which were deadly and forbidden by the United Consortium. Kitty's defense, which was true, but which she now realizes was incredibly dumb, was that she believed she was guarding a stockpile of food. Orlando, the rat, her lover for three years, had conned her into thinking he was helping the starving people of the region.

But on hearing of the approach of government troops he left her to guard the 'food supplies' while he went in search of 'help' to distribute the food to the starving Eritreans. She never saw him again. Her defense was dismal and resulted in an easy conviction. Every time she reviewed in her mind what had happened she was furious with herself for being so trusting and naive.

Classified as re-habilitateable with the new medical treatments, she was now waiting outside the Lunar surgical center for the 'treatment' that would restore her to 'normalcy'. According to numerous videos she had seen she was to be treated to the 'Intelliprobe', a nanoscale device which would be inserted into her brain and provide counseling and over-ride injurious decisions she might make. Apparently its nano-architecture would integrate with her brain. It sounded ghastly but her alternative was an indeterminate sentence in the Venusian prison complex and she had heard horror stories of that facility.

Kitty and the other prisoners were lashed with plastic restraints to one other so they would be treated in pairs and treatment, according to the vid, would place the probe into the region of the brain connecting the hypothalamus to the frontal cortex. Some thirty million neurons would be involved each firing off its message. Once in place you would be normal, according to the Consortium, and have none of those disturbing urges to do immoral or illegal acts . . . fat chance, Kitty thought, especially if you were innocent in the first place. Then what?

Kitty's partner was a girl with tattoos starting at her wrists and probably traveled along both sides of her body up to her face. If you can make out her features she was a normal looking young woman, maybe twenty years old. Kitty turned away from her not wanting to stare and imply she was odd looking but of course she was. Tattoos were frowned upon for the last hundred years.

It was too late, the girl edged her way towards her stretching her plastic restraints, apparently intent on being friendly. She moved up to Kitty's side, "What're you in for?" she said.

Kitty turned towards her and hoped that the shock of looking at her up close wouldn't register. She had tattooed spirals going around her cheeks and ending on the tip of her nose.

"Plotting a revolution," she said without batting an eye. It wasn't true but that's what she was convicted of. It sounded dramatic enough and it might give her some status with the girl or the other prisoners. But at this juncture what did status matter when you were about to get your head re-aligned with some kind of surgery. But then, admitting to herself that it might be good to talk to someone she added, "But I really didn't do that, I'm innocent. My so called boyfriend set me up."

"Wow, that's rough. You didn't do it? Wow! I know what I'd do in that situation. Zap 'em. But that's what got me in trouble in the first place. That's why I'm here," the girl said suddenly drooping slightly. "My name is Florella but everyone calls me, Ella."

"I don't understand. You zapped someone? What'd you do?" The girl shifted her feet and turned to the view port. "My boy friends, they two timed me."

"Well," Kitty said mystified, "That's bad but you don't get thrown in jail because of that. Who'd you zap?" There had to be more to the story. Kitty was getting interested and it was better than obsessing over the medical treatments she was scheduled for. Didn't she say boy friends?

"Yeah. It was bad. I hit them both with a stunner."

"Oh! But if you just stunned them?"

"Well, I thought I had it set on the low setting but the damn thing was on max. I didn't mean to, I'm dyslexic and read the setting backwards. That was my defense. It didn't work."

"So you zapped them. Wow. Both? Why both? If you had two boyfriends wasn't that cheating on at least one of them."

"No, no. They were my boy friends at the

8

same time, we were a threesome and they started taking an interest in each other and dropped me."

Kitty did her best to keep from laughing but really she killed two guys. In some ways though, it didn't make sense.

Many centuries back, Earth had legalized different forms of marriage and polygamy was normal these days. Polyandry was not, there just weren't enough men. Aside from being illegal, Kitty tried for an instant to imagine this tattooed young woman with two men but the images quickly became far too erotic. Kitty had no interest in more than just one man let alone sharing him with other women. For Kitty, Orlando was it for the last several years and, as far as she was concerned, enough for the next hundred years.

Florella continued, "I met some of those people who had the 'treatment' back on earth. They had the needles in their heads and they were the dullest people I ever met. They had no spark of anything. We used to call them dead heads. But I didn't have much of a choice. It's either this or twenty years in the Venusian prison stockade or on some other god-forsaken world."

It was unpleasant as Kitty looked around the room at the seated prisoners, a room full of future dead heads and she had to include herself in the mix. She looked at her new friend, Florella, who now was smiling brightly and began to feel sympathetic to this person. Kitty had spent her life on Earth and had never met anyone like this Ella or the Dead Heads she talked about. What a sheltered life she led and now she was scheduled for the 'treatment'! How could she have let Orlando double-cross her.

"They said this little medical procedure will get me on the right track. I'd be normal," Kitty said trying to alleviate her own growing fear. "I'm, Katherine, by the way."

"Nice to know you," Ella said, "But all those lawyers and the doctors, they lied. Normal, my ass."

Although she wasn't sure what normal meant either and for

sure she didn't know what the needles would do but considering the alternative of years in the Venus Stockade, Kitty's sentence of the'treatment' seemed like something she could do. But now, in her mind's eye she envisioned needles of all sorts and sizes. Small ones might not be so bad but what about big needles? And where would they stick them? Would they stick them? Out of your head? Or out of other body parts?

Appeals got her nowhere since Earth's consortium of governments had no sympathy for armed revolts. It was one of the worst of crimes, a thing of the past. She was considered a throwback to evil times when revolutions were killing thousands. The jury had found her guilty and she was guilty all right, guilty of being dumb. That damned Orlando, handsome, once the love of her life, had set her up to take the fall for his misadventures in arming the notorious but ill-fated Eritrean rebellion. She'd get even with Orlando someday. First she had to face a future with no good options.

A door opened at the medical lab side of the room and all eyes watched as a bulky woman came out. She had a white nurse's uniform on but from her build she could have been one of the security guards. She probably was both. She had a small locator in her hand and began scanning the room. Staring alternately at the device and then at Ella and Kitty, she then nodded to them, "You, DeLumiere, Corelli. You're next. The doctor's ready."

Kitty had forgotten she had an electronic identification-locator chip inserted into her neck. It was only the slightest of bumps but the bulge under the skin was a constant reminder of the judge's decision every time she looked in a mirror. Ella slid back on to her chair and stood up as the nurse approached. "Good luck," Kitty said, her voice trailing off as if she knew that there was nothing about this 'treatment' that needed luck.

"You too, Katherine...it won't be so bad," Ella said, and for an instant Kitty thought she sounded hopeful but this was a strange woman and it probably was just a front to hide a deeper fear.

The nurse shuffled over to the pair of them and took hold of their shared plastic restraint and, grunting loudly, led them both to the open door at the far end of the medical lab.

For an instant Kitty's thought was to pull away from this woman's grip but she looked fierce enough that neither she nor Ella certainly couldn't overpower her and the room had three other security guards. It would have been useless and where would they go anyway. It was the moon! She and Ella meekly went along.

There were stainless steel instruments strung out along one of the side tables in the medical lab, several gurneys and three robot arms dangling from the ceiling. Off to the side was a guard with his attendant array of stunners in his belt. One for long distance and one for up close in case some prisoner in the room became uncooperative. Most menacing was a display of needles placed near each gurney. At a computer console an older man sat, well groomed with a carefully trimmed beard and slightly balding head, he looked up at each of the two women, thanked the nurse and promptly snapped another plastic restraint on Ella's wrist. The other end was attached to the gurney. "A double murder, I see. Well, we'll have you in a more normal frame of mind in a few minutes." He then looked at Kitty.

"Ms. DeLumiere," he said as he flipped pages on his console in front of him, "I wouldn't have suspected you as a weapons runner." He read on in silence and then aloud, "Electro-shock grenades, sensitizer blasters. I think your sentence is relatively light. The stockade might have been more appropriate, but I'm not the judge."

Right, Kitty thought, just the executioner. The doctor, if that's what he was, seemed to have all the facts he needed. Protestations and claims of innocence wouldn't do much good at this late stage especially since the nurse had clamped a tight restraint on Kitty's left arm and drew it tight forcing her down to the gurney.

The doctor began mumbling commands to a computer and not

looking up, addressed both of the women, "Now, Ms. DeLumiere, Ms. Corelli. You'll find nothing painful about this procedure and you will be a new person in just a few minutes." As he said this he typed into his console a further series of keystrokes and then pressed a button ona unit attached to the gurney. The nurse flashed a sterilizing laser over each of their foreheads.

"This is the latest in medical treatments for your problem. The nano-transmitters are programmed for exactly these kinds of disorders. It will be so much better than the Venus stockade and you'll see the results are almost instantaneous."

Kitty didn't think she had a disorder. It was the legal establishment that had the disorder. That damned Orlando.

Her problem now was the robot which became activated. To the sound of whirring servo motors she saw it slide along a ceiling track and position itself immediately above her. As she watched the arm pivot, a thin needle projected from its grasp and its 'hand' twirled around, lowering itself to just above her forehead. The nurse had her other arm pressed against the gurney and the doctor slid another plastic restraint over it and tightened it pulling her down until she was lying flat. She began to struggle against the plastic but it held fast.

"I see you're the non-cooperative type," the doctor said, "We'll just lock you in place." Saying that he threw another switch and a band rose out from behind her, looped itself over her head, pressing her head back until she was totally immobile. She was locked in place. From the corner of her eye she could see Ella, on her own gurney, wide eyed, watching intently Kitty's struggle.

Kitty heard the frightful sound of the servo motors kick in again and could see the robot hand approach with its needle barely touching her skin.

"This is just the probe for the resonance scan identifying where the incision is to be made," the doctor explained as the robot hand scanned her forehead. It suddenly rotated and from the corner of her eye Kitty could see that a small drill had taken the place of the needle. The servos activated and the drill bit extended breaking the skin directly over her forehead, penetrating her skull."As I said, totally painless, correct?" the doctor said but Kitty could see that he was breaking out into a sweat. Was he enjoying this? She wasn't.

She could feel no pain but smelled burnt bone as the bit withdrew. Then the Intelliprobe swiveled into place.

Chapter Two

How clever these medical engineers are, Kitty thought, as laser beams had scanned her forehead and stopped at the place of choice. Its preference must have been sent to the computer circuit controlling the Robotic hand which gyrated until it apparently liked what the laser told it. It then proceeded to insert the intelliprobe into the hole in her skull it had just drilled. They're giving me the cure for which I have no disease, she thought. What if Ella is right and I turn into a deadhead? There didn't seem to be any way out though. It was really too late to take the twenty year sentence in the Venus stockade.

How many other people, how many innocents like me, have been treated this way? But then again, maybe it'll stop me from making wrong decisions like ever taking up with Orlando the Rat in the first place. She promised herself that she would not change and would stay Kitty DeLumiere, idealist, adventurer but maybe not so naive.

"There!" the doctor explained as Kitty heard the servo motors stop and she saw a collection of red flashing lights, diodes maybe. But she wasn't sure they were real or just in her head. "The probe is in the hypothalamus area of the midbrain and is now assessing her neuronal architecture." Clearly his explanation was for his nurse. "Once it has that information it...."

He never finished the sentence but was interrupted by a sharp snapping sound that came from Ella's gurney across the room. Both the doctor and the nurse looked over to see the guard with a knife in his hand hovering over Ella with the remnants of her plastic restraint dangling down. From the corner of her eye Kitty could see that Ella was free and was being helped off the gurney by the guard.

"What are you doing?" the doctor shouted "We haven't finished with her yet!" His nurse left her position by Kitty and charged over to Ella but she didn't get far as the guard drew his stunner and fired at her. She collapsed onto the floor. Through the corner of Kitty's eye she could see her lying there twitching.

In surprise, the doctor looked at his stunned assistant and raised his hand as if to threaten the guard, but only got the next shot from the guard's weapon. He too collapsed and fell to the floor but in doing so hit the computer control panel. Kitty felt a slight jolt as the servos ground away twisting the robot hand out of position accompanied by a snapping sound and a slight pressure in her head as if something broke...the nanoprobe? Was that damned invader still in her head?

Stepping over the fallen nurse's body, Ella said, "Let's get you off this thing," and rushing to Kitty she fumbled with the controls trying to loosen the head restraint on Kitty, finally succeeding. "These guys are the nutty ones. Are you okay?"

"I don't know," Kitty said massaging her wrists. "Did that thing pull everything out?" She rubbed the area of her forehead that had been insulted by that drill. There was something there but nothing to grab onto. "It must have snapped that damned probe off an' something's left inside me. I don't get it," Kitty said trying to regain her balance. The room seemed to be spinning or was it the probe or the anesthetic. She braced herself on the gurney and with Ella and the guard's help managed to stand. "Where can we go, it's the moon, right? There's no place to go." Ella put her arm around Kitty and the guard placed himself on her other side supporting her with his right arm. They lifted her off the gurney platform and led her towards the exit door of the lab.

She looked at her bloody hand and then at the doctor on the floor and wiped the blood off on the doctor's shirt and had enough to wipe on the nurses uniform.

"Souvenirs," she said. "Are they dead?"

"No!" the guard answered, "I only stunned them, but with enough juice that they won't remember any of this. We should get out of here, don't you think?"

"I think we've got a chance to get off this piece of rock," Ella said struggling with a still unsure Kitty. "My friend here Jason says a freighter is heading out in about an hour and we can hitch a ride. The Captain's his friend."

Finding it harder to maneuver on her own, Kitty gladly took Jason's shoulder. "I've got a million questions," she managed to say, "Like how do we get out of this holding pen?"

Ella laughed, "Katherine, right through the back door and it doesn't matter where we go but we gotta get out'a here and off this rock...fast. It'll work out."

The guard, Jason, unholstered his stunner and aimed it at the two women, Katherine looked at the stunner and the thought flashed through her mind that he would for some reason fire at her. Maybe this was some set-up to eliminate her.

"Just act like I'm taking you to a recovery center. Act like you just had the operation, maybe stumble a bit," he said smiling.

Kitty thought that stumbling might be the easy part. She was definitely not feeling stable enough to walk. Her only hope was to be able to hold together enough to get out of the treatment room and on to whatever Ella and this guard had in mind. He was a young man about Ella's age and seemed attracted to her. She must have worked some kind of magic on him.

With Jason's help passing the checkpoints was no problem. The guards knew Jason and with a little light banter let him through taking his two "prisoners" with him. At each new hallway there were new security stations but passing them went smoothly. It seemed to be

16

normal business. After the third checkpoint they began walking down a long isolated passageway. At mid-point, by a doorway, Jason stopped, looked around to make sure there were no witnesses and opened the door and shooed the two women through. It led to a stairway heading down into the depths of the Lunar Base. Being such a hostile place the engineers had constructed much of the Base underground.

"This is a longer way to the freight yards, but no-one ever uses it. The elevators are easier," Jason said as he closed the door behind them.

Ella started down the stairway but stopped and looked back at Kitty, "Are you okay, you look a little pale."

Kitty knew she was not alright since the walls had started to slowly close in on her, but even in her distorted mind she knew that escape was infinitely better than staying behind. Maybe later in a safer environment she could find some doc to get that probe or half a probe out of her head. Right now she had to live with it and hope there wouldn't be too many side effects.

"I feel a bit weak, but let's go on. We can make it. I mean I can make it." Kitty then gave a cursory nod to her left, "I mean me and this other person can make it. Who is she? Did she escape surgery too?"

Both Ella and Jason stared at Kitty and then each other.

"Katherine," Ella questioned, "are you sure you can do this. There's only us, no one else. I think that operation is getting to you."

Kitty looked around feebly and nodded, "Yes, the anesthetic. I forgot. Strange things." Forcing herself to hold her head upright, she continued down the stairs which fortunately were brightly lit. That seemed to bring a certain clarity to her still befogged mind. At the bottom of the stairwell they faced a passageway which seemed to go on forever. Feeling Jason's arm firmly around her waist she knew that in spite of bouts of darkness, at least in her mind, and then periods of clarity or consciousness, she knew she could continue, but the feeling that there was one other person with them remained. It seemed wiser, even in her half-awake state to let Jason and Ella worry about who that was. Whoever it was seemed friendly enough. She even seemed familiar.

The underground tunnel appeared to carry steam and air lines which according to signs posted every so often indicated they were going to the freight area. Even in her half-conscious state Kitty could see that they were approaching a huge room hundreds of meters across and a ceiling at least thirty meters high. Six parked ships were loading with crates being hauled around by fork-lifts on the ground and some suspended from ceiling tracks. The buzz of activity was dizzying.

Jason whispered something to Ella and loosened his arm about Kitty. "I have to see the Captain of that ship," he said pointing to one of the ships with the name 'Escadril', written in barely understandable letters, on the length of its main cargo area. That apparently would be their ticket out of this lunatic horror. Feeling somewhat stronger, Kitty nevertheless reached out to hold on to Ella's arm. She felt vaguely abandoned by her rescuer, Jason.

Jason headed to a large ship sitting on rails and facing the air-lock doors. It seemed to be in a warm-up mode at least by the dull red glow of its two fusion engines, one on each side of its main cargo body. There were large air vents on either side of the engines probably removing much of the generated heat.

Over the whine of several engines warming up in the port, and the roar of the air vents, Kitty managed to ask a question she had wondered about since the operating room. "Ella, how did you ever get this Jason to help you, us? And where are we going? Not that I worry about it. I don't care where as long as it's off this moon, but you're amazing."

"He's sweet, isn't he. I knew him back on earth. We had a thing going then and he still remembers. We are lucky." She looked up and Kitty swore her tattoos were changing shape. "An' I don't know where we're going but it's better than here."

"But why are you taking me along? I owe you a big one."

"Well you were the only person who'd talk to me since I got here. You seemed like a friend. Why not. None of us needs needles in the head."

This Ella has a depth to her that could easily be hidden by her looks, Kitty thought. Another reminder to self- not to judge so quickly.

Out of the crowd of technicians and stevedores loading cargo and milling around the Escadril, Kitty could see Jason walking quickly back towards them. He strode up to the two women

"They're heading to Jupiter, actually one of its moons, Europa. That's where I'm from, isn't that great. He will take us there but we have to be careful and not draw any attention to ourselves."

He bent down slightly and with a barely restrained smile, whispered in Ella's ear, which even in her numb mind Kitty could overhear.

"There are only a few crew members, but the Captain's given us a private bunk." Then noticing Kitty standing there, "and you too. Not with us, you've got a place of your own."

Kitty was relieved. She was dreadfully sleepy and needed some kind of bed and a compartment with these two in it would certainly keep her up all night. But there she goes judging and second guessing.

But Europa! The ice world! She had heard about that settlement. And Jason is from Ilandia, a city on Europa. No wonder he's excited. She had seen videos of the cities that were set up on that moon. Ilandia was the biggest. They looked modern enough but they all were carved out of kilometer thick ice and the temperatures there were hundreds of degrees below zero at least on the surface. How could they do anything in that kind of a place? But in some ways life there was far easier than being on boiling hot Venus. Cold you can work with. All those nuclear generators and power plants provided enough heat to melt out acres of ice and then they could break the water apart and get all the oxygen they needed. It all sounded strange.

But the colonies had been established there more than a hundred years ago. It seemed to work. Get used to the cold, Kitty, you'll be there a long time.

Perhaps the stimulation of new surroundings and the real possibility of escape from Luna gave her a spark of energy, enough that she managed to climb aboard the Escadril by herself. Once on board she was overwhelmed by its cargo area. Even though dimly lit she could see it was stuffed with crate after crate of insulation, snap generators, mining tools and other cartons she couldn't make out. Ella was standing next to her clearly impressed that Kitty had climbed the gangplank into the ship unaided.

"Hey, you. I think you're getting better already. Maybe that machine took most of that brain probe out of your head when he kicked it."

"Ella, you're an optimist. I feel something's still there. It's not too bad, but I think I have to crash sometime soon. I'm starting to see double again."

Ella looked around and then at Kitty. "You're seeing something aren't you? Someone? Maybe it's your spiritual guide. Ask them if we're going to make this trip in one piece?" Ella was serious. She must believe in such things. Kitty didn't.

It was not double vision that Kitty was experiencing; she knew what that was when she had caught Dengue fever in Africa. Rather this was a real woman just off to her side, just within her peripheral vision area. If Ella didn't see this person then what was happening?

"Now you've done it. This is what you get when you play with fire. You should have known Orlando was not for you." She spoke! The vision spoke! It was the woman! Kitty looked around and was certain no one else had said this and neither Jason or Ella reacted. The voice was familiar but she could not place it.

"How can you be so naive, Katherine, to let yourself be played for a fool. He suckered you in to take the ...rap, I think that's the right word, for what he was doing. What a ...rat. I'm glad we don't have

20

rats in Mondara." Whoever it was had decided this was the time to scold her for choices she made years ago. She had told Ella about her troubles but had never mentioned Orlando. Or did she? The voice, the voice. She knew who it was. It was her own.

Chapter Three

As Kitty was led on to the ship she heard the engine noise change from the hum of the warm up to a loud whine. If that was the beginning of the take-off sequence it was a welcome sound. Maybe she could escape from that woman who was following her. Her criticisms were getting to her and how could that voice be so much like her own?

Her guide through the twists and turns of the ship was Cody Williams, the ship's communication Officer. He was a young man, probably no more than Kitty's age, maybe around thirty. He had a neatly pressed white shirt on with the insignia of Aztec Lines, the owner of these freighters.

Another rumble reverberated through the ship.

"That, Miss DeLumiere, was the gangplank being secured. I think take off will be in a matter of minutes now. There are procedures posted in your quarters. Please follow them for take-off. And, we'd like you to remain in your room until the crew comes aboard."

Take-off! Kitty cautiously felt relieved. It meant they just might get off this rock before anyone found out what had happened. And then a bed finally in a room, a quiet time, by herself, relatively safe away from prison people. Now maybe she could come back to life.

Williams led her to her quarters which seemed to have all the essentials, mainly a sleeping cot, really a sleeping tube with heavy covers. Opening a closet in the room, Williams pulled out several grey almost leotard-like outfits hanging there.

"One of these should fit you," he said, "And you'll need the gravity boots too." He indicated several pairs of soft boots at the floor of the closet. "You didn't use these getting to Luna?" he asked.

"No, that was just straight forward. Sit in your chair and be quiet."

"I'm sorry," the young man said. He looked genuinely concerned and she wondered if he knew of her case, the charges against her and her defense.

"When we heard you were coming aboard I did read a summary of your trial," he went on, "I hope you don't mind, and from what was there you really should have been released. But I'm not the Consortium. They had nothing but circumstantial evidence against you. I can't imagine more of a travesty of justice." Kitty looked at him. A sympathetic soul here in outer space. She knew Cody Williams would be a friend.

Again the engine sound changed. "Once we begin steady cruising phase," he continued, "the magnetic gradient suits make you feel comfortable in zero G and they have adjustable pressure controls so your muscles get a workout like on earth. They can be underwear if you'd like. I know you didn't need anything like this on the trip to Luna but we're going a hell of a lot farther. Europa's far out there."

Kitty suddenly realized she was letting herself in for some major travel. Perhaps weeks in space.

"How long will it take?" she asked as Williams was about to leave.

"Oh, maybe six months, but a few of us hibernate for most of it."

Kitty felt stunned.

"How long?"

"The Captain knows exactly, but about six months. The time goes quickly once you're in hibernation."

It's like six months in solitary, she thought and she began to have that sinking feeling for having made perhaps, the wrong decision after all. Would it have been better to go through with the operation and be done with it. Be the happy little princess the state wanted. That thought didn't sit well with her.

Safely tucked in her sleeping container Kitty barely remembered the brief acceleration of takeoff. It was not nearly as bad as leaving earth, that usually reached five or six Gs. This time it was something like 2Gs and you could do that standing on your head. Still it was good having her own space all tucked in even though it was a room not much bigger than a closet back on earth. It had a small desk with a vid screen set up and off to the side a collection of service bottles labeled water, what passed for orange juice and one labeled protein. Enough to survive on. She wondered how that strange woman that came with her would get any sleep, the bed wasn't big enough for two. Then it dawned on her, the woman! She was still there and seemed to be sitting at the small table the crew had provided her. But was she really there? She stared down at the woman and wondered if this was a dream.

"You, who are you?" A wide eyed Kitty asked and half expected the figure to disappear.

Instead the woman with half open eyes looked up at Kitty,

"I was wondering when you'd come to life. I thought maybe you were dead. That would be such a waste. I was daydreaming. And by the way, getting away from that lunar hospital was probably one of the few smart things you've done."

"I was sleeping and..." Kitty didn't finish her answer when she realized the woman's voice was entirely in her head. "Wait a minute, who are you? What are you doing following me?" she asked out loud. "I must be dreaming."

As she stared at the figure she realized that the woman really did look very much like herself. Talk about being bipolar. The thought that she must be going crazy entered her mind. It had to be that probe screwing around with her brain.

"You're right! You must have a thousand questions and I'm sure my answers will not satisfy you but I'll try. I am following you, in a way, but only in your mind. Mostly in your visual cortex. My science people have explained this to me but I'm only a historian and I'm having trouble understanding all this too. But apparently we can communicate in real time. You and I can actually talk even though I live billions of your miles away from you. I don't know why we can but we can, apparently it's something to do with that piece of nano-scrap left in your brain. It's sending signals through the quantum scum...and don't ask me what that is. It sounds disgusting.

"For me it's the closest thing I can get to an experience of your world and not have to wait a hundred years after everything has happened. You know, the speed of light. It's always a problem. My name is CK1gRt but the closest you can get to that is Carg."

Kitty threw off her covers and slid out of her bed.

"No you don't...you're not in my head, you're right there, I can touch you," and she reached out to the woman's shoulder but she felt nothing. "I was right, I'm going crazy. Nuts! I should have stayed on the moon and had the whole treatment. By now I'd be back on earth feeling all good about myself. Now I'm nuts."

"You are not nuts. I had to look up that word...slang from ancient times...interesting." The figure of Carg looked around, *"They didn't give you much room here. You're squeezed in like a ...sardine? That doesn't make any sense either. Sardines have the freedom of your ocean."*

Kitty forgot for a second and explained, "No, sardines in a can."

Carg, the figment, continued, *"Oh! I see. And please forgive me for not getting the words fast enough. And I'm not getting your fashions right either. What I'm wearing looks terrible. I'm not sure what's appropriate in this situation but I think, according to those videos you've watched, I look better than you do."*

Kitty looked at Carg's image and she was wearing one of the latest fashions out of the Parisian scene. She looked much better in it than anything Kitty ever wore, but then she never did go in for fashion in the Eritrean desert. What does this hallucination expect?

"Tell me about your Orlando," Carg said sitting on the desk crossing her legs.

Kitty climbed back into her bed and pulled a pillow over her head.

"Come on, girl, what was it? Did he cast a spell on you. Some magic potion?"

Kitty pulled the pillow tighter over her head.

"No." she groaned.

"Well was he the ideal man, the epitome of masculinity? The perfect mate! I could understand it if he were."

"No, you don't understand anything about me...go away."

Carg raised her eyebrows. *"That's why I'm here. You're my subject."* She shrugged her shoulders, *"All right, you rest, I'll be back."* And she slowly vanished.

Chapter Four

From previous runs the bridge crew knew the daily routine of Captain Brace Adams. Today was only slightly different. He would run his fingers across his hologram projector and press a well-worn key. Projected in front of him would then be a small figure, no more than six inches high of a young woman. Dressed in a white summer dress and with her dark hair swishing from side to side, she waved to him and mouthed "I love you." He would press a second key and she would vanish. Cody Williams, sitting across the bridge and Sadoka Engstrom, the chief engineer, knew this ritual well. Ever since the accident, Adams had repeated it daily. They could see the image but said nothing. Business began after she vanished.

They were now almost three hours out from the Lunar base and both Engstrom and Williams realized this trip was not their usual run and it was not because of the magnetic storms in their approaching sector, they knew they were of normal intensity. It was the presence of unscheduled passengers that made this trip different.

"Captain, we're being hailed by the Lunar authorities," Williams finally said after the woman's image disappeared. Adam's looked over to his engineer,

"I expect they have a problem," he said with a slight smile.

"Yes, sir. It's an APB and they're looking for two escaped woman prisoners and one guard that appears to be missing from Moon

Base 4. They seem pretty excited about this. It's the first escape since the colony was founded."

With only slightly raised eyebrows the Captain glanced at Cody "Their first escape," he said "I used to be concerned about things like that where some agency gets in a bind mostly from incompetence on their part. If they can't keep tract of their people that's their problem.

Sadoka frowned, "it may be our problem, Captain."

"You worry too much, Sadoka. I worry more about getting top efficiency out of our engines," he said sharply.

Sadoka Frowned, "That, Captain, is my main concern." Sadoka knew that Adams was more and more troubled by his injured leg, a remnant of the incident years back and his temper was slightly more edgy these days. She continued, "But if those Lunatics give us a hard time...we might be facing some real troubles."

"I'm sorry Sadoka, you're right to worry. I apologize." He turned back to Williams, "What else did they say?"

"Because they've searched the base, and didn't find them they're sending a fighter out to board us. They think we might have stowaways. We were the only ship leaving in the past day." In response to a flashing diode, Williams turned towards the Captain, "Captain, the Commander of the Lunar fighter wishes to talk to you."

Adams turned to face the forward view console, "On screen."

The full presence of the Lunar Commander appeared above the console. He had his officer's uniform on, a bald head which certainly indicated how serious he was and he made a concerted effort not to appear cordial.

"Captain Adams, I am Commander Andrew McNeil of the Lunar Fighter Ace 12. We note you've received the APB that the Consortium has issued and since your ship left the Lunar Base shortly after the prisoners went missing, I'm required to board your ship for an inspection. There's a 91% chance the escapees are on your ship and our mission is to locate them and return them to the Lunar facility."

"Understood Commander. You are welcome and while we don't believe we have these people you are looking for we can still prepare you a cup of tea for your troubles."

"Captain Adams, this is not a trivial matter. One of the women, an Ella Corelli is guilty of multiple killings, the other, a Katherine DeLumiere has been convicted of arms dealings with violent revolutionaries. She is particularly dangerous if she reaches some of the unsettled regions of our outer colonies and there is a high reward for her return. The third person is a deserter from the Lunar Guard Force, a Jason Rheinland"

"I see, Commander. And would we qualify for this reward if we located this DeLumiere woman? "

"Well, unh... the reward would be split by all parties involved."

"Commander, as I've said I don't believe we have any of these stowaways but we welcome your visit."

The Commander nodded his head, " We expect to rendezvous in about two hours. Over and out," and the image vanished.

"Well, Sadoka, Cody, as I told the commander, we don't have stowaways," the Captain said leaning back on his chair and folding his hands in back of his head, "we have invited passengers. All right, they probably are the ones those Lunatics are looking for but I made a decision about those people more with my gut than my head. And now, as I do think about it, I would do the same. I owe the young man, Jason, a debt."

Sadoka knew that several crew members and the Captain's wife were killed in that accident years ago and someone named Jason was somehow instrumental in that rescue. The fact that anyone survived a crack-up in those temperatures was a miracle.

Looking at several images of her computer output, Sadoka presented the Captain with her vidpad, "At our present speed, that fighter will intercept us well before we get into   interplanetary space.

Maritime law says they have the right to stop us and if we don't cooperate ..."

"I know, Sadoka, they have the right to stop us anyway they can."

Sadoka continued, "And that includes firing on us. On the other hand, if we do stop for them and they find these stowaways we may all lose our licenses."

The Captain finished her sentence, "and be arrested and maybe lose our heads but I want you to know, if we're stopped, I will take the heat. You have nothing to do with this. It was my choice and my responsibility."

"Captain!" Cody stood up from his console, "I've heard the kind of treatments they've been giving out at the Lunar station. I was always opposed to that program from when I first heard about it. I always thought that program came out of the dark ages. The reports say it is an updated version of things like lobotomies... but we don't vote on what the consortium does."

"No, Lieutenant," the Captain interrupted, "I take responsibility. But for now, as long as these, unh...guests are here I suggest we treat them like any other passengers...although we may have to hide them in some strange storage spaces before we meet up with the Lunar fighter."

"I don't look forward to that," Sadoka said, "but I know some places on this ship that even I can't find one day to the next."

Cody Williams sat down at his console again and began reading. "It's not that simple. The two women were prisoners and from what I can glean from this report, they both were at the relocation center and have implanted transponders, surgically implanted, with a broadcast range of a kilometer, which means they can be located anywhere on the ship. I don't think we have anyplace with enough shielding to block their signal."

There was silence for at most a minute then the Captain spoke up, "You are right, they probably can be found anywhere on the ship. but, they can't be found if they are not on the ship."

"Captain, you're not thinking..." exclaimed Sadoka with a look of surprise on her face.

"Sadoka, you should know me better, I couldn't jettison a Europan flea into space, but how about if we send our guests on a space walk outside the ship. If that fighter Captain is inside the ship looking for our three desperados, the ship's outer shielding will block their transponder signal. After all it keeps out Jupiter's radiation, from infrared all the way up to hard UV. Let's call it a game of 'hide and seek', and the Captain can 'seek' all he wants, we'll just make sure 'hide' wins."

Chapter Five

Kitty sat in her cramped quarters staring at this woman who called herself Carg. All right, Kitty figured, if she is not real then she's a figment of her imagination. That's called awake dreaming or insanity. Whichever fits. But she's had dreams in the past where she asked herself in the dream whether she was dreaming. Usually the answer was no, but she really was dreaming. It was all too confusing.

"Katherine," Carg said, this time appearing in a different outfit one Kitty vaguely remembered from a fashion site she was looking at several months ago. *"I think you need a better explanation of why I'm here."*

"That would be nice, it might keep me from going completely crazy."

"You are not going crazy," Carg admonished. *"For some reason maybe related to that piece of nano-scrap in your head, you've become a receptor for this mental excursion I'm on. Once our engineers discovered that you were accessible they assigned me the project of studying your civilization. It has something to do with what you people call quantum foam. Once you're down to that level, they tell me, the speed of light limit doesn't apply I thought I explained that. The uncertainty principle allows that. Up 'til now we've been able to observe Earth's transmissions, television, and radio but because we're so far from your world.*

"My world!" Kitty exclaimed. "You mean Earth!"

"Yes, your world, Earth. I live a long way from you. It's in a star system you people only give a number to. But it's not to say we

haven't visited your world. I checked our history files and found that we have! But that was more than five hundred of your years ago. Your popular press referred to us as little green people. Kind of insulting."

Kitty was trying her darndest to take this all in. "That's how you know about us?"

"Yes." Carg answered, *"But our latest information is over a hundred years old. That's because we are a hundred light years from your world. The council ruled out more trips to earth because of budget cuts and frankly you were so behind us at the time they didn't think it was worth it. That's why this connection with you is so great. We are in real time and it doesn't cost very much although my superiors are still complaining about their budget. They ruled out actual visits.*

I've made your world my specialization, your language, culture, habits. And I might say they are interesting. I will probably get an entire book out of just you alone."

"Let me get this straight. You live on another world, a billion miles from us and somehow you've got a way of getting into my head and then you're going to get a book out of me. That's weird. Should I be flattered or what?"

"Yes, my people will love your story. I've learned your language. It didn't take too long and what's in your brain storage area is fantastic. You have been around."

"No! I haven't! You can read my mind? No fair! No way!" Kitty began to blush as she thought of her life and some embarrassing incidents. Could it be that damned probe! It has to be that. It broke off and is doing strange things. What the hell is quantum foam?

"But if you're real and I'm not nuts then your world must really be way ahead of ours. I mean you visited us five hundred years ago." Kitty rubbed her fingers across the slight lump in her head where the drill had done its thing. Whatever was happening it had to be the probe.

"If that's the case, how come you look like me? And how come you speak with an English accent," Kitty found that unlikely.

Carg laughed and then said, "*Kitty, I'm taking on a form that you can handle. It was in the visual cortex of your brain. It's like your memory storage room and it seemed handy but I haven't mastered your modern accent yet, your auditory cortex is harder to get into. I've learned English from all those British videos you've watched. Give me a few hours and I should sound better. Should I take someone else's form? Someone you've seen before?*"

Kitty thought about this for a second and replied, "Why not just be yourself?"

"*I can't because you've never seen me or any of the people on my world. You have no idea what we look like. Really we are a lot like you, only minor differences. And there are no images of us in your brain for me to assume. Also, we're a little taller than you humans.*"

"Well of course you are! What differences? How come you're wearing better clothes than I have?"

"*These are the fashions you admired just a few weeks ago,*" Carg answered. "*The images were still in your brain.*"

Carg was right. She had been looking at clothes like that when she was in the prison waiting for her treatment. This was getting more fantastic rather than less.

"Well, what do you look like?" Kitty cautiously asked. "Are you like those little green men...hey! Are you a guy or a girl?"

"*I'm more girl than guy, according to what I know of you people, but really we're only a little different. We have DNA like yours, but ours is triple stranded. I can't see how you people get by with just one other kind of person. We need three of us to get together to reproduce. It's much more difficult to find two others that agree, that way it slows population growth. From what we found from your video reports, that was going to be your earth's main problem. Besides with three we get much more in the way of umm...immune defenses, and other things.*"

34

"I'll bet. Wow!" Kitty thought that this Carg had something more in common with Ella. But she kept that thought to herself--if that was possible.

Carg was right though. Earth still hadn't slowed population growth. Every bit of land had a premium on it. Overcrowding was becoming a nasty problem and in a few cultures cannibalism was becoming more and more acceptable. That's one reason they did away with Earth's prisons. The land was far too valuable and scarce and space transportation was relatively cheap.

Was it possible to keep thoughts away from this creature if it could enter your head and read what's there? "Do I have any say in what you can do in my head. Maybe I don't want you to know everything I'm thinking."

"Kitty. By the way I like your name, just tell me and your thoughts will be off limits, it'll slow me down a bit, but if it's alright with you I can still use your visual cortex. That lets me see what you're seeing."

Kitty thought about this for a moment. "You mean everything I see you can see? Why would you want to do that. My life is boring an' if the lunatics find me you'll see nothing but prison bars. If we do escape I'll be in hibernation for months, won't see anything."

"Hibernation!" Carg exclaimed, *"Just a minute...I had to look that word up...that means you'll be asleep for all that time?"* She looked disappointed.

Kitty was about to pursue the conversation when she heard a knock on her door. Both Kitty and Carg looked towards the door.

"Yes, I heard it too. I'm getting that auditory thing working," Carg said. *"They won't be able to see me. I'll be in contact,"* she said as she stood, waved goodbye and slowly became more and more transparent until she vanished before Kitty's eyes.

"Miss DeLumiere are you there?" the Comm officer Cody Williams called out. Inside the room Kitty whirled about but Carg indeed was gone. Was she ever there in the first place?

"Yes!" she finally answered. "Come in." Kitty was so confused about the presence and then absence of Carg that she was beginning to think anything was possible and that maybe the Captain had decided to eject her and the others into space just to get rid of them. She caught her breath as the young officer entered. He introduced himself again, Cody Williams, Communication Officer. Waiting behind him were Ella and Jason.

Williams stepped inside Kitty's room, elbowing his way past the small desk they had provided her and quickly looked around.

"I thought I heard you talking to someone," he said quizzically.

"Don't worry about her," Ella chimed in, "that operation she had did a deed on her. She's seeing things."

" No, no!" Kitty protested "I'm fine. But every once in a while I do talk to myself. It's nothing." She knew it was not *nothing* but if this Carg was real it was amazing and they wouldn't believe her anyway.

"I hope so," Williams said. We're going to need absolute quiet from you three for awhile. We expect a visit by a Lunar fighter. When it gets here, in a few hours, they will probably scan for you two and if they contact those damned implants of yours every one of us will be in trouble. You all have to be moved..." he hesitated before continuing, "to an area we hope will be electronically safe."

At that point Kitty had a thought thrust into her head, *'Ask him why we just don't out run them'*. Kitty sensed it was not something she would have thought of, it had to be that damned Carg. Was she listening to everything?

Kitty gave up trying to resist and finally blurted out, "Why don't we just out run them?"

Williams smiled and explained, "It's a fighter they're sending and they have twice the engine power we have. We couldn't outrun them if we tried and it would certainly tell them we had something to hide. That would be much worse for the whole crew when they did stop us."

Kitty had her own thought, "But if they do find us then it's back to the Lunar Colony or worse."

Williams tilted his head and answered, apparently the best he could, "I'm sorry but we'll try our best to keep you hidden. The Captain has suggested a hiding place that appears perfect. I don't believe anyone will find you there." He didn't elaborate.

Chapter Six

The Escadril was already nearly two hundred thousand miles away from the Lunar base and in a normal run the hibernation subroutines would kick in and open sleep compartments for the crew. Everything would be set on failsafe mode with the electrostatic field and the radiation guns about the ship's exterior protecting them for the most part from rare micrometeor strikes. The Captain and crew could go into hibernation for the next six months if they wished. Any other deviations from normal ship operations would activate their wake cycle and they could tend to the matter in minutes. Still, Adams had only done the hibernation stint a few times. He disliked it and the feeling of having missed six months of his already uncertain life kept him off balance for the rest of the year. After the accident several years back he preferred to stay awake and do some thinking or rather try to straighten out his thinking, and possibly sort out matters left undone from the accident.

But he knew this trip was not a normal run. He had perhaps foolishly taken on board two escaped prisoners from the Lunar Colony and the young man, Jason, who was certainly AWOL or at worst guilty of desertion, but he was a friend.

On his right he noticed Sadoka, his engineer, busy staring at her compscreen. She turned away from the screen and looked at him, "Captain, all joking aside," she said. "If they are looking for your friend Jason and find him out there , we'll all be in some serious trouble with the Lunar authorities." Somehow Sadoka could sense what was bothering him. "And", she continued, "Earth will probably cooperate and . . . "

38

"I figured they would."

"I hate to bring it up," she continued, "but that rescue on Europa, what was it, five years ago? Well, they'll find it was this same Jason that got you out, remember, I was there, and someone will argue that you may have even planned this escape. Especially if your friend has it on record that he wanted a transfer out of the Lunar base. I've heard that these Lunar stints are not any prized assignment. You need someone to put it into words for you, Captain, then maybe it'll sink in- - with all due respect , Sir."

Adams began to stare at the ceiling but he knew she was right. He hadn't thought of the downside of his decision only that it was right. Jason, almost frozen himself, had rescued him after the crash years ago. He also tried to find the Captains wife in the wreckage. But there was no sign of her, no communication from her after the crash, so everyone concluded after eighteen hours of searching that she must have lost her shielding on impact and slid into one of the many crevasses. After an hour with no shielding and if her thermal suit failed it had to be too late for her. Temperatures that day were way lower than two hundred below zero. It was only a stroke of luck, if you could call it that, that Jason was able to get to the Captain before the he froze solid, although the Captains leg sustained frostbite and destroyed some major nerves and there was other neural damage that couldn't be repaired. Jason was only a teenager then but fought with his superiors to keep on searching. They didn't let him and that's what got him into trouble.

Now was it only a matter of waiting to see if the Lunar Police would locate the prisoners? The chances of finding them on the outside of the ship were small yet if they did find them, it was a bad position to be in. He chided himself for not thinking things through and gave orders for the crew to deny any knowledge of their passenger's presence, he alone would take the heat. That seemed like a fair bargain. He had put himself in danger with the Solartime

Commission and Lunar authorities by allowing their escape. It was well intentioned but foolish.

Looking back towards Sadoka he noticed that her compscreen seemed to be flickering rapidly.

"Anything Sadoka?"

She stared at the screen, didn't look up but answered, "I don't know. Someone is scanning our ship's schematics and operating manuals."

The Captain got up and looked over her shoulder. " Anyone is entitled to look at that manual. Is it a problem? Where's it coming from?"

"No sir, no problem. But it's coming from the engine room. Sensors say there's no-one there now, strange."

****

Comm Officer Williams led Kitty, Ella and Jason to the lower level of the ship where one of the crew members, Lex Andrews, took charge. Lex was a handsome young man, maybe Kitty's age, dark brown hair, and introduced himself as the ship's integrity officer which meant, he explained, that he was responsible for the hardware features of the ship like the exterior controls and hull itself and had responsibility for all the mechanical components of the ship. Kitty was impressed.

Before heading back to the bridge, Williams admonished them to be as quiet as possible once they were boarded by Lunatics from the Fighter and if they were discovered they were to claim to be stowaways.

Lex marched them to a large room with what seemed like airtight doors on the front and back. He announced to all three of them, "Welcome to the space discharge unit. I think we'll have ourselves a bit of an adventure trying to hide from the Lunatics. I'd like you all to put one of these suits." He opened a metal door to a large closet in which a collection of uniforms were hanging." There are different sizes, pick one that fits. I'll help you get them on. While the visitors are here we will do a short EVA." He took one himself and stepped into it and locked his head bulb in place.

To Kitty they looked a bit strange especially with that large bubble for your head. How could they hide in something like that? It seemed awkward at best and what does space discharge mean? The Captain and Lex must know what they're doing. And what does EVA mean?

The lunar fighter would be there in no more than an hour and if they found any of them, even in these suits, unless it made them invisible, she very probably would be back on Luna with that same doctor with his shiny new needles only now with much more security and poor Jason would be in trouble with his desertion. Somehow she felt Ella would survive.

At least she was thinking now and free of these images of imaginary people. Imaginary? Was Carg really a figment of her distorted mind? She tentatively thought of the name Carg again as if to call on this creature. Carg, are you there? She repeated but nothing. It was all in her imagination. Her alter ego didn't appear and in some ways Kitty was disappointed. But then she heard a voice say, *"You'll have to excuse me--bathroom break."* Kitty felt a sense of relief that maybe she wasn't imagining all this but Carg was real, yet who in a normal frame of mind has a friend that can appear and disappear in a whim. Wasn't that a sign of the psychotic mind? But why would a Psycho have a friend who had to go to the bathroom? And then she realized she was thinking of Carg as a friend.

"Carg," she thought, *"we're about to be boarded by a lunar fighter ship. They're looking for me, us. If we can't outrun them and if they find us here, me and Ella, we'll be doing that prison stint I mentioned before. The Captain says he has a better way of hiding us, that's why we're putting on these suits. I think he wants us off the ship!"*

41

"Off the ship! But you should be all right in your suits. Isn't that right?" She stopped abruptly, *"I think your Captain has a very good idea."* She continued, but then said, *"I'll be leaving you for a while, but I'm sure the Captain won't throw you off the ship and let you drift forever into outer space. I have an idea. Be back, don't worry,"* and she vanished.

Kitty felt her anxiety level rising and with it her heartbeat. If Carg knew what was going on, why didn't she tell her and why did she have to leave so soon? Can you even expect behavior like that from your alter ego?

Lex was adjusting the head piece on Ella, "Now I've got you all tethered into my lifeline so we're all tied together."

"Why do we need that?" Ella shouted, Kitty could see an alarmed, hysterical Ella who began flailing around in her suit. "Why are we into these suits?"

Jason, who already had his suit on and bubble adjusted, took her by the arm, "Relax, Ella. We'll be all right. I've been through a space walk before. I've got you." Startled, she looked at him wide eyed through her head bubble, but even Kitty could see she didn't really relax.

"Space Walk!" Kitty certainly didn't relax either as she heard those words. She knew that was coming and wasn't counting but she was sure her heart beat doubled, again.

"You will all be okay, just keep your feet on the skin of the ship. The line will keep you from floating away," Lex said. After checking all their suits, he pushed a button and Kitty heard the sound of the rear doors closing and of motors running. Pumps! They're pumping out all the air! We'll be floating away! The pumps became silent as the ten foot high door facing space itself slowly opened revealing a black starlit sky and she knew what they had in mind. *How fast can your heart beat without exploding?* She thought.

"This way, ladies and gentlemen," and Lex proceeded out the door. She felt herself being pulled along by the tether into the void.

42

She wasn't really used to the magnetic shoes but once outside the ship she totally lost her orientation, of what was of up and down. It was now only stars and blackness above her, with only the ships outer shell and a few scattered landing lights for her bearings.

Chapter Seven

Lieutenant Cody Williams looked up from his Comp screen, "Captain, the Lunar fighter is approaching. No visual contact yet, but we do have video. They'd like a word with you."

"I imagine so, all right, on screen," Adams answered knowing this was the beginning of their problems. These guys were good and with no scramblers to hide the transponder signals, it didn't look so good for the Escadril or those kids. He seemed to think of Kitty, Ella and Jason as kids, although in an earlier day he might have been interested in Kitty. She seemed like the more interesting of the two women. But today, he felt more like the wise captain, protective of his passengers. And, of course, Ella's history of having shot two of her boyfriends didn't make her attractive in the least. Somehow Jason should know of that history.

The Central image projector lit up with a snowy image, which clarified as they watched. The Captain of the fighter turned to face Adams directly, "Captain Adams ," he said slowly.

"Yes," Adams answered hoping he could lie effectively. "Captain McNeil again. We are approaching rendezvous. Please keep your present speed and we will attach at the Level 1 hatch. The Lunar authorities have double checked and there was no response to their scan for their transponders on Luna. It is unlikely the devices were deactivated and they certainly couldn't have gone far from the facility. The latest data is that it is 94% likely the stowaways are on your ship. Have you located them?"

"Level 1 hatch is activated, and no, we have not located any unaccounted for personnel...stowaways as you say." Adams noted that the fighter Captain seemed to be all business, a typical military-civilian interaction. He thanked the Captain as the image went back to all snow.

If Lex managed to hide their guests they might get away with it, even with that 94% probability. But if McNeil's technicians locate the prisoner's signals there would be not much sympathy for him as Captain nor for the crew and probably not for the stowaway story. They would take the escapees and allow the Escadril to proceed to Europa but a return to earth might be problematic. That's when the Consortium and the Maritime commission would throw the book at him and maybe his crew. For himself, he knew he could take what punishment they might offer but his crew had no part in his folly. The only way out would be to stay on Europa the rest of his life and that he couldn't imagine ... an ice world with bad memories? He had been to Europa a few times before , the last, that ill-fated freight run where he lost his wife.

The Europan cities were comfortable enough even though they were constructed a mile or more under the top ice layer. There seemed to be too much compression and tectonic activity in the first mile of surface ice but tidal action from Jupiter was enough to warm the lower levels of ice to allow large scale construction projects without everything freezing up on you. Small atomic furnaces and fusion torches allowed the rapid expansion of the tunnel network and then cavern construction followed by vaults that housed whole cities. The upper ice layer provided protection from most of the radiation the moon was bathed in and provided insulation from meteor strikes. An ideal place in the outer reaches of the solar system especially since major industries were interested in the deposits of gold and rare metals discovered there when miners finally hit the rocky core.

But still...an ice world and memories of the crash were still too intense. Adams was born a Terran and that seemed to be the kind of world he wanted to live on. He preferred looking at mountains, not icebergs, although he couldn't climb either one. By now there were entire generations of Europans who knew no life other than the world of ice. They might be happy there, not him. But still his wife was out there someplace... frozen or worse. The thought of her body poisoned with radiation still gave him the chills.

Adams turned to his engineer, Sadoka as he heard her mumbling, throwing switches and entering computer commands.

"Sadoka! Report!"

She still seemed to be preoccupied with series of entry commands.

"Captain. . . I . . . " more switches thrown, "I've lost control of the engines . . . no, it's still there!" More switches. "The engineers at the Lunar station said they'd tuned up the engines but, this is all new. No one briefed me on these changes."

"Sadoka, we did leave early...you know, hot passengers," Adams said as he moved from his chair limping over to watch as she tried more commands.

"No, I have engine control but it's telling me that the efficiency is low, only 6 percent, and I should switch to a pulsed mode. That doesn't make any sense. When we got to the Lunar base we were running at 92%." She looked up at the Captain who looked back to her with raised eyebrows and an expression which said, 'Well, what do you think?' "I've never heard of a pulsed mode. What the hell did they do at Luna?" Sadoka continued to stare at her screen, "It's offering me choices now-- nanosecond pulses and microsecond intervals--and then an automatic setting?"

The Captain thought for a second and said, "Do nothing now. Let's get this Lunatic visit over with and then we can try to understand what happened. Damned engineers."

****

"Kitty, what are you doing here? This looks like the baggage compartment. Did they finally kick you off the ship?"

Carg's image had once again formed in Kitty's mind. She was now wearing a green and white pants suit, tighter fitting than Kitty would have worn. Not only was she looking more chic than Kitty ever did but she swore she looked five pounds thinner yet she was using Kitty's own body. That wasn't possible.

"We're going outside the ship. We're hiding from the Lunar fighter that just got here. The Captain thought that they wouldn't find us if we hid outside the ship. Maybe they wouldn't detect these locators Ella and I have implanted." She unconsciously placed her hand by her neck.

"Smart man, your Captain. Is this him?" Carg was looking at Lex.

Kitty thought she saw some amorous look to Carg as her alter ego fixed her eyes on Lex.

"No, Carg, that's Lex and get your eyes off him, he's mine." Kitty's reflex action startled even herself. Here she was hiding out from forces that would do her in if they found her and she's somehow protective of her own desires. But there was no reason to be so concerned. She and Lex had barely met, only enough to have him help her with her space outfit. Maybe, her unconscious thinks we are going to get out of this and is thinking of the future. Or is Carg really Kitty's own alter ego.

"All right, but I think you're missing out on a real . . .Hunk . . . I had to find the right word for him. If you don't want to mate with him, let me have a go at him. You can sleep through it all." Now her alter ego was being sarcastic.

"Carg, Go! I'm thinking about saving my life and you're thinking about sex. Go!"

"Alright," Carg said, *"But I'll be back."*

"Why do we need these suits?" Ella shouted, Kitty could see an alarmed Ella who began flailing around in her suit.

"Relax, Ella. I've got you." Startled, she looked at Lex through her head bubble, but even Kitty could see she didn't really relax. Her eyes were wide with fear. "We'll be alright," Lex said, "I've been through a space walk before."

"Space Walk!" Of course, outside the ship means a spacewalk. Kitty certainly didn't relax either as she heard those words. She wasn't counting but she was sure her heart beat doubled again.

Tugging on the steel tether line Lex said, "You will all be okay, just keep your feet on the skin of the ship. The line will keep you from floating away." Being weightless inside the ship was one thing, she was used to that from the ride to the moon, but now facing the infinity of empty space was very different. Her magnetic shoes were working but this Lex could shut them off any time he felt like it and she would float off into the void. He wouldn't do that would he? He might if the Captain wanted to get rid of them . . . released into space where they would freeze dry and float out into the vastness to be discovered millennia from now by some space alien.

Their electronic connection allowed them to talk to each other but all she heard was Ella screaming in her suit to the point of hysteria.

Kitty's worst fear seemed to be coming true, Lex would be the henchman who would cut the line and push them off into empty space. But to her relief he turned to face his trio of followers, "Calm down, you're all safe. Now keep your feet onto the ship's hull and just step or slide along." Lex's voice came through clearly enough and he demonstrated by squarely putting his foot down onto the metal surface and sliding ahead a few inches. Barely able to contain herself but wanting to follow every instruction to the letter, Kitty did as Lex suggested and found that her feet comfortably stuck to the surface and she could lift them off at will or slide. Maybe she wouldn't have to fly off into space after all.

"Now your suits have all been energized to give a magnetic attraction to the ship's skin so you will feel the pull almost like gravity. Just like in the ship," Lex said as he stepped away from the space door onto the ship's surface. "The Captain wants to   keep you hidden when the Lunar fighter gets here... for at least a few hours. So follow me." She heard him through speakers in the glass bubble.

Yes, people have been walking in space for hundreds of years, but not Kitty. Weightless inside the ship was one thing, outside the ship was entirely different. Here if you leaped off you would keep on going forever. Inside you simply would hit the walls of the ship and bounce, hard but you would still be there, a little bruised but inside the ship.

In as soothing a voice as he could muster Lex got closer to Ella who was wide eyed looking out of her bubble,

"Ella, you're safe, I've got you tied into my lifeline and you can't fall, we have no gravity here."

The logic of his words may have been lost on Ella who let out a primal scream which unfortunately they all heard. Then he added "You can't fall!" He turned back to his trio, "all right space walkers follow me. I will go slow because I have to re-attach the lifeline every meter or so." He held up the carabineer clips to show them and made an elaborate show of attaching the clip to rings attached to the ship's hull.

"We attach three of them to ensure safety. It's slow but safe." Inside Ella's head bubble they could see that she was trying her best to calm herself and follow along.

Kitty was last in line and she watched the procession in front of her as they slowly made their way across the hull following Lex who was continuously clipping the carabineers on the line and then off. It looked like a funeral procession but they managed to cross much of the body of the ship and seemed to be heading towards the engines. According to Lex they were silent at the moment since the ship was in glide mode.

He explained, "We will take up residence inside the engine compartments. Their shielding should protect us and block any signals from those transponders you women have." He continued as they approached the engine housing, "I have been in here many times. It should be perfectly safe."

Kitty thought for a moment, what does he mean 'should be?'

There was no sound of the approaching Lunar fighter until contact was made with the entry doors. Then the clang of their locking rings reverberated throughout the ship and told those four curled up inside the engine housing that now was the time for absolute quiet. Would the Lunar police somehow detect them even here on the outside of the ship. Lex was confident they would remain hidden.

But the thought reverberated in Kitty's head, 'It should be safe?'

Chapter Eight

Captain Adams and his officers, Lieutenants Williams and Sadoka, stood in welcoming formation while Captain McNeil and five of his men entered the Escadril from Hatch One.

"Welcome aboard," Adams said as the team approached.

"Thank you, Captain," McNeil acknowledged. "My men are equipped with Multirange Detectors and with your permission will search the ship for these stowaways."

Good, Adams thought, this military type is all business, the sooner he finishes his search the sooner they will leave. And he knew McNeil didn't need permission but it was a diplomatic thing to ask for.

"You have my permission," Adams said, "but we've already searched and we have found no stowaways or any other un-accounted for personnel on the ship. I will be interested in your findings. Perhaps our search wasn't thorough enough."

"Perhaps. And your permission includes the officers and private quarters, I presume?" McNeil said , "I have the schematics of your ship."

"Of course," Adams acquiesced, "That's all publicly available."

McNeil then met with his first lieutenant and his men scattered to the different corners of the ship while Adams and his officers relaxed back on the bridge. Sadoka went back to scanning the new messages that were appearing on her vid.

"Captain," Sadoka said, not taking her eyes of the vid screen, "the new engine algorithms seem already entered into the control protocols. From what I can tell we've got much greater capabilities. The engineers on Luna never filled me in on everything they did."

"Take Care, Sadoka. Let's not take any action until McNeil and his crew leaves; we don't want to . . . disturb their docking."

"Certainly Captain. I've already put a lock on the computer. It's steady as she goes."

"Thank you Sadoka, 'Steady as She Goes' sounds good." but Adams knew that from now on his life would be quite different from what it had been the past sixteen years. Laura was out there frozen for sure down in some crevasse or locked between sheets of ice but he had to find her. His hope, a distant hope, was that she was not being subject to Jupiter's relentless radiation. If Jason couldn't find her it might mean she had fallen into some deep ice valley hidden from the barrage of x-rays and gammas. He had to try to find her body and settle this five year old question in his mind. Put it to rest.

****

As the trio of escapees huddled in the engine compartment one hour turned into two then three before they felt vibrations throughout the ship that meant that possibly the Lunar Fighter was leaving. Lex had been plugged into one of the sockets on the skin of the ship listening for some word that reentry was safe. He now nodded his head and plugged their com wires into his.

"They've gone," Lex said with a smile that was visible through his glass headpiece, "We can return. You people make me proud. You're space walkers."

Ella seemed to finally relax and before anyone else, began to climb out of the engine housing. Lex took her arm, "Ella wait, I have to go first, we still have to connect ourselves as we go."

"Katherine, does that mean you can go back inside the ship?" Carg asked appearing next to Lex.

"Yes, Carg, finally," Kitty answered. *"Now get your hands off Lex."* Carg's image had placed her hands on Lex's rear end. Although Lex didn't seem to feel any of this it made Kitty uncomfortable to see. Was Carg acting like the extra-terrestrial she claimed to be or was it Kitty's own unconscious getting ideas. She never quite could be sure which it was. Carg withdrew her hands. *"You are too sensitive, Katherine."*

With the 'all clear' from the Captain, the four of them, began their long trek back to the loading lock. It was slow going with Lex again re-attaching the links again every six feet but the pace allowed Kitty to look up from the surface of the ship to the stars which filled the sky above her. One of these stars was so much brighter that the others. It had to be the sun but at this distance it could barely cast a shadow. She suddenly felt lonely. She knew 'up' was a relative term because there was no reference world to judge from . . . there was only the ship.

At one point Kitty had an almost uncontrollable urge to jump off into space. Much like the feelings she had back in Eritrea when she would advance to the edge of a mountain cliff and glimpse empty space below her for a thousand feet. She never jumped, but the urge was there. Here she could go up into space and avoid her legal troubles and the law. The law that she felt had so mistreated her. She wouldn't have gone too far being tethered as they all were. Fortunately she didn't give in and knew being tied to the others she would have just floated around like a balloon. Lex would have planted her feet back down, but she vowed to continue fighting and if she had to live the rest of her life on the ice world she would. Jason loved that place in spite of his trouble with the military so it must have something going for it.

Ella seemed to have finally accepted her situation even though Kitty knew she was emotionally a wreck, at least from the way the tattoos on her nose kept changing colors. She had learned that was an indication of Ella's mood.

It was good to have Jason along. He had a steady hand and helped Ella make her way from the engine cowling back to the loading dock. One or two times she had tugged on the tether and pulled herself off the ship, floating uncontrolled but Jason set her down.

He seemed to have a good relationship with her although Ella's preference for other partners might be trouble down the road. But for now they seemed thick with each other.

Once inside the loading dock and with the doors closed, Kitty could see the air pressure gauge slowly rising and finally heard the hiss of the air being pumped in. On the upper wall she relaxed when the gauge read 'Air Pressure: Normal'.

Twisting off his head bubble, Lex smiled and said, "There people, you are experienced space walkers. That was a difficult EVA and you all did very well."

He was being very generous. Kitty didn't feel as if she had done well but if she didn't fly off into empty space it was a success.

"Kitty, you're back." It was Carg and in some ways it was comforting to hear her voice even though it was her own that Carg was using. *"I tried to get to you a few minutes ago but all I saw were stars. You were way outside the ship. That made me nervous."* Kitty could see Carg walking beside her on the way to her quarters. She always wore an outfit that was so much nicer than anything Kitty had. This time it was tight fitting pink slacks and a blouse to match. Fortunately, Lex, who was walking beside her didn't notice Carg's image--or did he?

"You were nervous!" Kitty thought, *"Yes, we were outside and for a good reason. The damn Lunar police sent a ship up here looking for us. That's why we went outside. I think we're okay now."*

"That's a relief." Carg continued, *"I wanted to tell you that I couldn't keep our conversation going for months at a time if you went into hibernation so I asked for a little help from our engineers. My people tell me that they looked into your ships control algorithms.*

54

This tub of a ship was so mis-tuned that with the changes they could make, they could increase the ships range by two hundred percent and the speed by almost ten times. I told them to do it. I hope I didn't do wrong. From what I could tell them they said we'd be at our goal in a few days. You call it Europa. What do you have planned then?"

Kitty had no answer. If Carg's meddling was real it might be disastrous or it might be a blessing.

****

Sadoka Looked over her engine control panel and carefully, gingerly tapped in the command for the automatic pulse mode. "As per your orders, Captain, it's in pulsed mode. Amazing. We're still here."

Sadoka was transfixed by the blinking lights of her console and the comm-screen indication of increasing speed.

"The fusion engines are firing in nano second bursts and the fuel injectors are in phase and ...Captain our speed is increasing."

"I don't understand why the Lunar people didn't fill you in on their changes?" Adams reached for the arms of his chair to brace himself. "You feel that...gravity?"

"Not quite. It's a constant acceleration. It just feels like we are in a gravitational field."

The computer interface with the accelerometer showed the speed increasing ...160,000...163,000...165,000 miles/hour and no limit in sight. It couldn't be an error not with the sensation of gravity they were feeling. But speeds like those indicated were not possible at least before the lunar adjustments.

"Captain the gravitometer is reading lunar normal gravity...about one sixth earth and it's stable. "And it's not a fluke, the instrumentation seems to be working if you can believe the numbers. Lieutenant Williams interrupted,

"Captain, we had visual contact with the fighter but lost it. They faded out of visual range. We must be going a hell of a lot faster than they are."

The captain smiled, "it isn't bad having this kind of capability." But speeds like what the instrumentation were indicating didn't seem likely. The latest was now 177,000 m/hr.

"This doesn't seem possible. But Sadoka, if we have acceleration," the Captain slowly added, "We must be burning fuel, that could get us into trouble."

Sadoka looked from gauge to gauge to digital output, tapped a few to see if they were working.

"No, Yes. . . we are burning fuel but in a pulsed mode, I've never seen anything like this before. The fuel bursts are nanoseconds long and only microscopic amounts are used in each burst and they're all in phase." She tapped a few more gauges, "Temperatures are in the safe range and the engines look stable. We won't use anything significant in fuel and if we keep on accelerating we'll be near Jupiter in days, not months. Slowing down just means going into reverse thrust when we get there and make our landing. There seems to be an automatic mode for that, even."

Captain Adams was intent on the same gauges that Sadoka was reading. "The engines can't do this," he insisted.

"Captain, they are." She countered, "And it all looks stable as if they were designed to do this. I give credit to the Lunar engineers, I didn't think they were this good. Damn engineers."

Chapter Nine

Draping Kitty's space suit over his arm, Lex watched as she started to remove her lime green jumpsuit.

"I've been wearing this suit for weeks now. I really am tired of it," she said as she struggled with the top trying to get it over her head.

"I think I had better give you some privacy, Katherine," he said backing towards the door.

"Don't you leave me now," she said, "Help me get out of this prison underwear, it's strangling me."

Lex tugged as best he could and finally she pulled the top over her head.

She turned to look at him holding the top of her suit. "I'm tired of running away, you just plan on spending some time here." She now was down to the barest of prison underwear. Lex hesitatingly bent over her bare shoulders and then kissed her on the back of the neck. She turned and grabbed him by the arms and held him to her. "What was that for?" She asked, not quite surprised by his interest.

"Nothing, you look so beautiful," he answered as his hands caressed her shoulders and moved further down her body.

"I didn't know you were interested in such nothings. Then you can just stay here and tell me more." Saying that she leaned backwards onto her bed and pulled him down on top of her. He did not resist. "I thought you were all business," she said, putting her arms around him.

"Not when the most beautiful girl in the world is before me," he said and then kissed her again.

Suddenly Carg appeared, *"Katherine! Let me. Let me take over. He looks like fun."* She had almost nothing on and was sitting on the bed next to the two of them.

"Carg, you get out of here. He's mine. Get lost!" Kitty tried to think as intensely as she could.

Carg turned her head and looked at Lex. *"At least can I watch?"*

Lex by now had his shirt off, *"Get lost--I mean it."*

Just before Carg vanished, she turned up her nose and said *"Spoil Sport! You know that's a very useful saying and ..."*

Kitty commanded in her thoughts, *"Get out of here!"* And she did, vanishing without another word.

Kitty breathed a sigh of relief, which Lex may have interpreted otherwise, but at least she had Lex to herself undisturbed for the next few hours. They both took advantage of their time alone.

****

Those few hours with Lex were just what Kitty needed after months of mistreatment by the consortium and Penal system. Before that she was with Orlando, the Rat, and she now knew he was a schemer and a user. Lex doesn't seem to be any of these; he was romantic and he seemed honest in his feelings. At the very least he was good in bed. Maybe that was all that was needed until she knew him better.

Carg was no help. If that creature could get into her head she was getting into her sensual side. Right now she needed to be smart and advice from Carg was questionable. But she was still unsure if the image of this creature, 'Carg', was real or was an awake dream, or even a side of her own self. A walk about the ship might clear her head, if that was possible. At some point she knew she'd have to have that piece of the nanoscale probe removed but she doubted if the ship's doctor, if they even had one, would be able to do the surgery needed and she was sure that probe was easier to put in than take out.

The thought of someone scraping around in her brain looking for what was left of the probe was disturbing enough from someone who was skilled, but a ship's surgeon or those ridiculous med-bots, who usually treated ingrown toenails and stomach bugs, was absolutely frightening. That broken probe had to be responsible for the image of Carg she was seeing and someday she would have it removed although that 'figment of her mind' was turning out to be interesting. But was she more than that? She hadn't settled that yet.

Then again, did she really want to get rid of Carg? After all it did seem she was an alter ego of Kitty's, even if she was picking up more of her erotic side than her rational side

As she walked about it dawned on her that they had a natural sense of gravity. No longer did she feel as if she were floating. The feeling with magnetic boots was quite different from real gravity. She wondered how they did that.

Did Carg do something that provided gravity or did the ship's engineer, Sadoka, figure out how to do it?

Already several days on board the ship fighting magnetic boots and trying to walk normally, the return of gravity was a welcome treat. Katherine relaxed and wandered about the freighter deck, passing bulkhead after bulkhead, areas where the cargo was stored, the ships kitchen and then an area set aside as an observation deck. Its video screens opened onto a panoramic view of the heavens. A view of the stars might help and give her some perspective on her situation and Lex. It had two rows of chairs facing open space and an ever growing image of a bright disk that had to be Jupiter. Another woman, a rarity on this almost all male crew, was seated there sipping on a drink. Kitty sat across from her and introduced herself. The woman, who looked about forty, with nice dark hair, smiled and offered her hand. She was dressed in a flimsy blue ankle length dress, something Kitty didn't expect anyone to wear on a freighter.

"I'm glad to meet you. I'm Mira Landusky, call me Mira," the woman said. " I heard the Captain had picked up two women on Luna.

It's good to finally talk to you. At first I thought you two were competition and going to be working the crew."

Katherine knew what that meant. Working the crew was a euphemism for being a sex worker. These were girls, and sometimes young men, hired by the ship owners to be Pleasure Pals for the crew who sometimes spent a year on a transit if they didn't go into hibernation.

"No, I'm just a passenger," she protested. "Katherine DeLumiere, you can call me Kitty. I'm just trying to stay as far as I can from both Earth and Luna. The Captain was a life saver."

"So the rumors are true, you and the other girl escaped from the Luna prison. You were supposed to have that new brain operation? It sounds scary."

It was amazing how fast rumors spread. Katherine smiled,

"Well it was. It wasn't painful but the thought of it was more frightful that the surgery."

She didn't say this to this woman, Mira, but she thought Carg was one of the side effects of the operation.

"Finally we get to meet another woman." Carg's image floated before Katherine's eyes.

"You keep quiet, Carg. She'll think I'm crazy if I start talking to you."

"All right, but she sounds interesting...she's a sex worker? That fits right in with the book I'm writing...find out more."

"I don't want to find out more. Be quiet. You're one of the side effects." Katherine thought trying not to look exasperated.

"It was supposed to turn us into a good citizens," Kitty said as she picked up the drink Mira offered her, "but we managed to break out before they finished. I always thought I was a good citizen but the courts on Earth thought otherwise."

"Wow! Good for you." Mira raised her glass as if to toast Katherine. "But you've still got your prison suit on. You're never going to pass for a good citizen wearing that."

Katherine looked down at her outfit, the same lime green outfit she's been wearing for the last two weeks. "This is it. I haven't anything else. We left in kind of a rush."

"I can imagine," Mira said. She put her drink down and stood up. "Look, Love, you're a bit smaller than I am." She seemed to be studying Katherine. "Actually I've put on a few pounds, but I have three or four outfits that would fit you and I don't know if I could ever get back into them. They're yours if you want them. Certainly they'd be better than your prison uniform. Come on, I'll show you."

"Take her up on that, new clothes...you really need some. What you've got is terrible so ...un- Chic." Carg would not stay out of her head.

"Carg, I told you to be quiet. I know I need new clothes, just stay out of it."

Undoubtedly Mira's Pleasure Pal profession had perks. Her cabin was much more spacious than what Katherine had and the outfits Mira offered were better than most things Katherine had even on earth. She feared at first they might be too sexy for her but that wasn't the case. Apparently Mira's attraction was not in what she wore.

Mira could see Katherine was looking longingly at several of her outfits.

"These are beautiful Mira, but I couldn't buy them, I don't have any credits."

"Katherine." Mira held up her hand as if to say stop, "They don't fit me all I can do is throw them out, take them. When we get to Europa maybe you can do me a favor some day. Buy me a brandy. Don't worry about it. But, you know, you'll need some kind of income when we get to Europa. Have you thought about it? Any Prospects there?"

Realizing that survival was another matter, Kitty demurred. "I have to think about that," she said, knowing it was a major problem lying ahead of her.

Realizing that she had nothing, Katherine accepted

Mira's offer and carted an armful of new outfits back to her room. She looked around her small cabin and thought what a difference there was between her small, barely maneuverable room and Mira's. Well, some professions have advantages but also disadvantages like strange men in her bed. But then again she had memories of Lex, those of Orlando were slowly being wiped out. And new clothes always gave her an optimistic outlook on life. Her alter ego would be pleased.

Chapter Ten

The great ball of Jupiter filled more and more of their view when Kitty and several of the crew members gathered at the observation area to see the coming attractions. At their distance the moon, Europa, looked like a shiny tennis ball floating by Jupiter masking out only a tiny fraction of the great disk with its bands of colors and at times the view of the giant swirl of the storm spot on the surface.

"That's it?" Ella asked. "I can't believe it. We're going to live there for the next umpteen years."

"It's a frozen ball of ice! I can't believe it either," Kitty said as both women sat there transfixed by the view of their next home.

"Lex says it's not so bad once you get to the cities," Kitty said thinking they should at least try to make the best of it. "He was born there, that makes a difference."

But she was not so sure herself that she could survive there. Not so much financially but she was so used to the lush African Veldt with all that grew there. That had been her home most of her life, now she was faced with... ice.

"The men might be fun there," Ella said. She was trying to look on the bright side. "From what I've heard there are not that many women."

"You see, Kitty she's thinking positively. You're the anthropologist. You should be studying men too." Carg's disembodied head had suddenly appeared.

"Carg, anthropology is the study of mankind not just men. And I have bigger problems that just giving you some thrills. I don't want to spend my life on that frozen ice cube either. And I was having a nice talk with Ella until you butted in."

Carg frowned and disappeared.

Kitty turned to look at Ella who was staring at their future home, "But aren't you and Jason a couple. At least that's what I thought."

Ella continued to stare at the white disk of Europa, "Jason is great," she said, "but I think I have to dump him."

Eyebrows raised, Kitty looked at her, "Care to explain that."

"I mean it. He's a good guy, honest, strong, and sexy but I think he's already thinking of settling down, you know kids, chickens, white picket fence and he's thinking about staying on this frozen ice cube. I know me. My tastes run to something more exotic. In the long run, I would only disappoint him."

In her mind's eye, Carg's head appeared again, *"You were right, Katherine. Your first impression of this girl was correct. She is a good spirit and seems to know her own self. More than I can say about some other people."* Before Kitty could get what she thought would be a quick witted response`, Carg's image disappeared. She tried to keep her dissatisfaction with Carg to herself. She turned to Ella.

"If that's what you think best, I support you. Maybe I can talk to Jason."

"That would be good Katherine, you take him."

"No, no. That's not what I mean. Maybe I can make this breakup easier. Have you told him yet?"

"No, I will before we go to the Captain's dinner." She looked at Kitty, "You are going, right?"

"Yes," she answered. "You know Mira gave me some clothes that didn't fit her and I think one of the outfits is even too small for me. It might fit you. Come on I'll show you."

With new code in the ship's computer system and the ever increasing speeds they were at, the crew was totally preoccupied with preparations for the Europa rendezvous. Kitty saw Lex every evening for the last week after their space walk and the Captain perhaps once in the last week, so it was a pleasant surprise to receive an invitation to dine with him. That was a privilege. The Captain's table always sounded so exclusive and a relaxed evening with hopefully good company was a welcome break. Usually she ate in the galley with Ella and Jason. They were fine company and she ate with them whenever possible but they would disappear back to their cabin as soon as they finished leaving her to make small talk with some of the crew, mostly a rough lot.

In the past three days Kitty had worn three of the outfits that Mira had given her. In that time she had been approached by at least four crew members to see if she would spend the night with them. She explained that she wasn't in the Pleasure Pal business but that didn't seem to impress any one of them. They all figured she was just bargaining for a bigger fee and they offered to double even triple what they were paying Mira. She still refused but it was tempting with the last very handsome stevedore who offered her over three hundred credits. That was enough for her to live on for a month. It just wasn't the business she wanted to get into and besides there was Lex.

Yet what work she could find on Europa was still an unknown. Carg was not helpful in that this 'figment' kept urging her to accept some of the offers the crewmen had made. She explained it would make good reading for her study of Earth habits. In fact she had offered to take over, use Kitty's body and let Kitty sleep through it all. This seemed like a workable solution to Carg, but in the end, to Carg's disappointment, Kitty decided against it.

"Just how are you going to live?" an exasperated Carg asked as Kitty was packing what few possessions she had in preparation for the arrival on Europa. Carg had appeared dressed in one of the fashions, a tight fitting pants suit, that Mira had given Kitty. Not

having the luxury of a full length mirror, Kitty admired the outfit seeing it on someone else even if Carg was only a vision in her mind. Carg was using Kitty's body but somehow she looked slimmer in it than Kitty might have. That was what she would wear to the dinner tonight.

"Carg." Kitty answered, *"We'll find something even if it's being a waitress. I've done that before."* Carg seemed at times to be acting as Kitty's more sensible self and at other times an irritating, sarcastic nuisance. How could this figment from another world take her down a notch every once in a while. The last time she appeared she was wearing the red, low cut outfit that Mira has just given her and claimed that she looked better in it than Kitty did. That's nerve, Kitty thought, from a figment, no less.

But Carg had a point that she couldn't get past, what would she do on Europa? Mira had given her an info cube with a hundred credits on it and addresses of several places she might find work. Most were waitress type jobs and one of them had another kind of work, it was for a Madam Canzioni's place as a Pleasure Pal, something Kitty so far had rejected. She hoped she could stay away from that line of work.

At the Captains quarters she pressed the entry button. The door opened and to her relief she saw that Ella, Jason and Sadoka were already there sitting at the table as was the Captain. Both he and Jason stood up as she entered. Coming up just behind her were Cody Williams and Lex. Kitty tried to smile equally to both Cody and Lex.

"Ah, Katherine, Cody, Lex, please come in," the Captain said and lifted up a glass and offered it to Kitty. "Venusian Brandy, I think you'll like it."

Dinner was a pleasant start to the evening. Since the trip to Europa took less than two weeks and food had been set aside for many months of travel with the old propulsion system, there was no rationing. It was a feast.

The Captain got down to serious talk after the last brandy was served.

"And you three miscreants." He pointed to Jason, Ella and Kitty, "The good news is that Europa doesn't have an extradition treaty with Luna or Earth. The early colonists on Europa knew that settling that place would take some hardy souls and made it easy for certain individuals, tough people, to emigrate there and not have earth snooping around after them. What matters to the Europan authorities is you behave yourselves on their world, although it's a pretty loose world."

Kitty looked at the Captain in surprise, "You mean we're free?" she said looking first at Ella who had an equally surprised look on her face, and then at Jason.

"From what I understand of the law, yes, but there's nothing free about living on Ilandia. You will still have to earn a living." The fact remains, however," he said nodding to Jason, "that You, Jason, left the Lunar Rangers without asking permission."

Jason smiled and said, "Captain, you are being too polite. I asked plenty of times but they said, no. So I deserted. My term with them was for a year and they changed it to eight years. They never asked me a thing, just did it."

The Captain raised his glass to toast Jason. "But Jason, you risked your life pulling me to safety in the accident."

Ella, sitting next to him and Katherine, both with raised eyebrows, turned to Jason. Adams continued, "It was about five years ago. Right? That counts for much."

Jason stared thought for a second and then said, "That's right 2462, I think March."

"Yes, not quite springtime, if you can call it that at two hundred below zero." The Captain continued, "We were making a shipment from earth and we lost control of the retro rockets . . . couldn't achieve orbit. We didn't burn up but we hit the ice hard. I think all of us had our suits on but on hitting the ice shelf some of us scattered onto the ice and lost temperature control." He seemed to choke on his last sip of brandy. "I got thrown out . . . and Jason got to me in time. You were on some kind of patrol?"

"Yes, I was with the Ice Rangers on a standard exercise and we saw your ship come down. I was just lucky to be there."

Adams continued, "We still lost two of the crew and I never saw my wife, Laura, again. They tell me we were exposed to at least 200 degrees below for about twenty hours."

"Did the Captain say he lost his wife...she froze out there?" Carg had appeared.

"I never heard this before, Carg. Be quiet."

"Captain," Jason interrupted, "I tried."

"I know, Jason, I got the reports of the rescue and what happened when you tried to get out there and keep searching."

"I'm sorry, Captain.."

"I know, Jason, but that got you in trouble with the military, didn't it."

"They wouldn't let me go back out there and keep searching. My suit had another sixteen hours on it and we knew right away that there was one more person missing but my commander refused. He ordered me to stay put. That's when I hit him. He didn't take it too kindly. I was young and I suppose hot headed. That's what got me into trouble. My military stint was extended to four years on Luna and then another four years in the Centauri system. I think they thought more time in the military would make me a better soldier."

Jason continued, "There were so many crevasses out there, some so deep we couldn't see the bottom. But I thought I saw skid marks leading off. They wouldn't let me follow them."

"Jason, you did what you could, but I think you'll have to keep a low profile when we get to Europa."

Adams refilled his glass and passed the brandy flask to Sadoka sitting to his right. "That accident happened a while ago and I've finally made a decision. Actually several decisions. I'm leaving the Aztec lines. That's the major one."

Startled, Sadoka looked at Adams and placed her hand on his arm, "Captain, what will you do? I didn't think you had any great love for Europa. Will you stay here?"

"I don't hate this ice world," he said.

Kitty noticed he grimaced a bit when he said that. "But I have other things to do." Then he said no more. Kitty knew that everyone at the dinner table wanted to ask Adams what he was going to do but they must have all felt if he wanted to tell them he would.

Chapter Eleven

Just as Lex had explained, Robie experienced the sequence. After the third signal she felt the loss of gravity and the magnetic floor activate. In a short time she, Ella, Jason and several of the crew she recognized gathered at the debarking area. They all heard the thud of the shuttle docking clamps, pumps working away to provide a breathable transition atmosphere and finally the airlock opening to reveal the shuttle interior with its neat rows of seats.

Strapping herself into her seat she found to her surprise that Jason sat next to her while on the other row of seats across the cabin Ella sat next to another of the crew members, one of the stevedores. On Kitty's other side Lex sat. She sensed, not totally unexpected, that there now seemed to be something different between Jason and Ella. They must have talked about their relationship, always a tough conversation.

"Oh this is exciting, Kitty. We've got Jason on one side and Lex on the other. Two men. Are they going to fight over us?"

"Carg, will you settle down. Lex and Jason are being gentlemen and it's not us, it's me. You're the illusion. I'm real."

As Kitty thought this, she saw in her mind's eye, Carg move over and sit next to Lex. Her hand wandered over his tight fitting pants. Apparently it didn't register with him but he blinked once or twice and Kitty wondered if he sensed something.

Now she was getting embarrassed and a little bit jealous. Wanting to give Carg an angry look. Kitty decided that she couldn't do that without giving Lex that same look.

Instead she focused her inner attention on Carg and commanded, *"Carg, get back here"*. Carg looked over to Kitty in surprise, frowned, gave Kitty a haughty look, squeezed Lex's butt one more time and faded away. Kitty felt pleased with herself. Maybe she finally had some control over this person or illusion or alter ego.

With all aboard the shuttle Kitty could feel the rapid acceleration as it un-clamped from the Escadril, descended quickly through what Lex described as "not really air" but mostly a thin atmosphere of ammonia and hydrogen. They finally entered the tunnel system heading to the Ice World's Central Customs area. Lights flashed by as they descended and Kitty felt a surge of excitement. As long as she stayed on this planet, or really moon, she was a free woman and no one was looking to arrest her. While the presence of her alter ego was still with her, Carg maybe could be handled. Or perhaps things would not be exciting enough for this strange illusion and Kitty's dull life here would make her lose interest.

"I've told you ten times that I'm no illusion." It was her again. *"I'm as real as you are. It's just that I'm billions of miles away. Where are we going now?"* She was back.

"Carg, I don't know whether it's good to see you or not but you've got to behave."

Kitty thought. *"We're going to Europa and heading towards customs and since I don't have anything to claim we sure should go right through."*

"We'll that's the problem, isn't it." Carg was beginning to sound sarcastic, *"You have nothing. You're going to starve and then where will I be."*

Kitty wondered if all the creatures on Carg's world were as self-centered as Carg. *"We will survive, there are lots of things I can do. I can be a waitress or a fry cook. I've done those things before."*

Carg, still looking like Kitty, brushed her hair aside, *"Well, here I am on my world trying to convince my supporters to spend a small fortune on this communication we're doing and I'm going to be observing a fry cook. In goes the steak, out goes the steak, in goes the steak. A good profession but that's not exciting. I'd rather you do more of this interpersonal communication stuff that Mira does. That'll give me some insight into human personalities and appetites."*

Ruminating over this bit of advice, true in some ways even with its sarcastic nature, Kitty still wanted to keep her principles and self respect intact. With Mira's help financial and otherwise, she should be able to find some kind of work, hopefully not in Mira's profession in spite of Carg's wishes.

Kitty's extra-terrestrial experience was so far limited to the Moon relocation center but she preferred to put that out of her head and concentrate on this ice world which was as different as anything she had ever seen.

Their shuttle descended to the ice surface and then into a mile long tunnel through the surface ice and every few hundred feet or so the Europans had ingeniously installed thermometer gauges. At the surface, where their ship landed, the temperature read 217 below zero and slowly rose as they descended until they landed at customs where it read a comfortable thirty degree above zero. That had to be Fahrenheit, didn't it? Or is that Centigrade?

From what she understood the entire city had small Thorium nuclear furnaces at strategic locations keeping every part of the city in the comfort zone. Much of their comfort had to do with the active insulation that faced the walls of ice surrounding the city and Captain Adam's freighter was hauling tons of that material, an essential part of the city's future.

As the passengers were leaving the shuttle, Lex leaned over to Kitty and whispered, "Don't go too far. I'll help you get settled."

She felt she could trust Lex but she wondered if she could trust herself "Once outside customs. We'll get together," she said.

As she picked up her collection of clothes that Mira had given her, Jason leaned over and said. "Katherine, I have to talk to you. I need an older woman's advice."

Kitty tried not to react to the "older woman" part of what Jason said, but it got to her. Here she was only barely over thirty but of course Jason was only in his twenties as was Ella and this probably had to do with Ella.

Carg appeared as Kitty was leaving the shuttle. *"See, you're missing out on life's experiences . . . older woman. And you call yourself an anthropologist."*

Chapter Twelve

As expected, Customs was not a problem and leaving the entry port, Kitty, Lex and Jason walked arm in arm out into the brightly lit streets of Ilandia. Contrary to what Kitty imagined this was no frozen colony with icicles hanging from the street lamps but seemed like a normal, busy cosmopolitan city with air taxis rushing to meet them, people walking from business to business. It seemed like a normal city. The only thing missing was a sky but the city had constructed a vast dome overhead with twinkling lights. To Jason and Lex this was a familiar sight. Home to them.

Lex raised his arm and pointed to a building off in the distance.

"There! That's the United Energy Corporation. They've got generators all over Europa, cutting through the ice ,warming the city. I bet you could find a job there."

For once Kitty felt that maybe her world wasn't ending here on this frozen world. Maybe there were opportunities besides being a waitress or joining Mira in her business.

Jason was enthusiastic, "This is a place where new beginnings are possible," he said. "My great grand-parents settled here hundreds of years ago. They were pioneers"

Kitty, thinking of Ella's decision turned to Jason and repeated, "New beginnings, Jason. You too."

Jason bent his head lower. He got the message, "Right, I have to remind myself of that."

Kitty knew he was still enamored of Ella but she also knew he had enough strength to break that fascination and move on.

She looked over to Lex who now had a more serious look about him and was intent on one of the air cars that had pulled into the taxi lane. It was not a taxi. One man jumped out of the car and waved a small instrument at them, the newly arrived passengers. To Kitty this looked exactly like the locator device the nurse had used in the Lunar facility to identify her. She felt the weak but definite tingle of her implanted transponder being activated. The man checked its reading and pulled out a rifle stunner from his jacket... and aimed it at Kitty. Lex saw this also and before Kitty could think he shoved her to the side exactly as the stunner fired. Kitty fell, but as she did she smelled the scent of burning flesh and saw a disembodied arm fly off into the distance. Collapsing on the sidewalk she felt Lex's body fall onto hers. The stunner must have been set on Max and to her horror had burned off Lex's arm. Another stunner blast filled the air but it was Jason who had fired. The assassins head flew back as Jason's beam hit it straight on. The second man in the car jumped out and aimed his stunner at Kitty but she instinctively had already retrieved Lex's weapon and she fired at the man hitting him in the chest. Before he collapsed she could see the other side of the street through the hole her stunner had made. So much for a new start in the new world of Europa.

Stunners are a strange weapon. Their beam on low power simply disables a person but does little physical damage. On high power, Max, for instance, it has tremendous impact and can disintegrate human flesh and actually sear flesh cauterizing the wound so there is little bleeding. People survive stunner wounds even with missing limbs, so too Lex but not her attacker with a missing head.

Lying on his side Lex turned to her, "Was that you. You got him?"

"Yes, Lex, both are gone," Kitty said as she stared at his blackened armpit. "We will get you to a hospital right away. You were hit. You saved me. Why would they do that? It had to be me they were after!"

Lex looked at her , closed his eyes and said, "Yes, everyone wants Katherine," and he passed out. Kitty thought, 'Everyone wants me...dead or alive.' She looked up and saw Jason hovering over her.

"Get help, Jason," she yelled, "Lex needs a hospital. He's got to make it."

"He will," Jason said reassuring Kitty, "I've seen wounds like that before and he'll be all right." A crowd was gathering now that the situation looked harmless and the shooting had stopped. Jason yelled to them, "Get an ambulance. This man needs a hospital. NOW!" Several of the onlookers reached for their commlines and in a matter of seconds they could hear sirens in the distance.

Jason helped Kitty up from the sidewalk as the ambulance arrived and, of course, a crowd gathered gawking at a wounded Lex. Finally the medics began loading an unconscious Lex onto a stretcher. In the distance a different kind of siren rang out. "The police," Jason said and with Kitty slowly backed out of the crowd. "Let's get out of here. They're going to ask too many questions."

"We can try this address," she said doubtfully,

" Are you sure it's right? Canzioni's," he asked after Kitty had given him Mira's info disk. "I know that place," Jason said as he and Kitty slowly wormed their way out of the crowd. "Are you sure this is where we should go, Canzioni's?"

The police van had arrived and there was a spirited conversation with the medics, police and several of the bystanders yet it appeared that none of the witnesses could or would exactly say what had happened or who was involved. They certainly didn't point in Kitty and Jason's direction. It was either two or three men or two or three women? Those who were witnesses had backed away and disappeared into the pedestrian crowd. The police looked around the bystanders now almost twenty or thirty and a few times in Jason and

Kitty's direction already well distant from the incident, but took no action towards them.

"Canzioni's is a rough place," he said.

"Jason, this is the address Mira gave me, it's my only contact on this miserable place. What's wrong with it?"

"Well a lot of rough characters go there. That's where some of the working girls are. I used to go there . . . to watch them . . . it was fun . . . when I was a teenager."

Kitty observed a slight blush on Jason's face but knew better even in her half hysterical state than to pursue that one, but Mira was a friend, one of the few friends on this planet and she felt she could trust her. She had so much more experience and maybe she could help out in some way. It was a new world and someone, somewhere had to help.

"Katherine, you are in a terrible state. What did I miss?"

"Carg. I don't need you now."

"Yes, you do. Talk to me ...you've got to calm down. What happened? The last time I left you, you were on the shuttle. I had to take care of things on my world. My bosses keep telling me that my work, this communication we're doing, is too expensive. I'm fighting them off...the money grubbers. What happened to you?"

"We, Lex and me and Jason, got out of the landing port and someone tried to shoot us. There were two of them and I think they were aiming at me, but they got Lex."

"What? Lex is dead?"

"No, but he lost an arm and then I shot one guy and Jason shot the second one."

In her mind's eye Carg raised an eyebrow. *"Wow, two shooters. You are more important than I thought. My boss will fund this work for sure. Why did they do that?"*

"I don't know! I don't know!" Kitty was fighting back tears of fear.

Kitty's thought conversation was interrupted by Jason who sensed that Kitty was in some sort of turmoil.

"Katherine, you're safe. They won't find us, certainly not here. We're safe for now."

It appeared Jason was right. The air taxi had left them off at the Canzioni address that Mira had given her. It was a quiet street on which sat a row of houses in styles ranging from the 23rd to the 25th century. The Canzioni address had an engraved brass sign on the door that said,

'Abandon All Troubles, Ye Who Enter Here'

Before Jason could ring any kind of bell the door opened and they were greeted by an older blond haired lady,

"Welcome to the Canzioni resid--" She said but stopped and reached for a shaking and sobbing Kitty and put her arm around her. "You my dear have come here with many troubles, I can tell," she raised her arm indicating the entire house. "Everyone can tell. I'm Madam Canzioni." She led Kitty into a foyer and sat her down on a small red sofa set against the entrance wall. With tears streaming down her face, a wild eyed Kitty certainly looked a mess. Her hair was stringy not to mention the bits of burnt flesh stuck here and there, just from rolling on the sidewalk behind poor Lex.

Madam Canzioni went on, "Whatever your problem, we can help. We know some of the best doctors in the city..."

"I don't think I need a doctor, I just shot somebody," Kitty cried out.

"Well then, that's not so bad." Madam Canzioni continued unfazed, "They probably deserved it. And some of our clients are the best lawyers in the city."

Mira was right, Canzioni's was a desperately needed refuge and maybe Madam Canzioni could help although Kitty didn't know how. Why did those gun-men pick on her and how did they know she'd be arriving at the entry port? And now they were both dead, will that be the end of it? Or were they assassins or maybe this was standard life on this forsaken world. It couldn't be a random shooting. Could it?

Jason introduced himself and further described the incident. On hearing his young masculine voice three girls came charging down the stairs.

The first one down, a young blonde girl, anxiously cried out ,

"Is he a customer? Mine!"

The other two rushed ahead of her and approached madam Canzioni. One spoke first, she was thin with mouse brown hair,

"No fair, Stephanie doesn't get this one, I do. She always gets the rich ones, I want this handsome one."

The third girl sidled up to Jason and ran her hand through his hair.

"Come on now, let him choose. I'm the best."

Madam Canzioni raised her hand in an attempt to silence the girls. "Ladies, we have an emergency here, this is not a business deal, and relax. Can't you see that this poor girl..." she stood next to Kitty and placed her hand on her shoulder, "is in need of help. She shot someone, so did this young man. You ladies have to keep your hormones in check until we figure out how to help them." She looked down at Kitty, "Now, tell us what happened. You have my word," and she looked severely at the three girls, "that no-one here will speak of this to anyone else."

Rubbing the last tear away from her face and taking a deep breath, Kitty felt that Mira was right, this is where she could find some security and be safe, at least for a while. She then told of the Lunar hospital and the bungled operation, the escape and how Mira had helped her and finally in the last few hours, their landing at the space port and the shooting.

Kitty looked over to Jason who was standing there by her side but with the dark haired girl leaning on his shoulder.

"Jason has been my hero through all of this. Without him I'd be dead or worse." As she said this the dark haired girl gave a blushing Jason a noticeable hug and looked at Kitty,

"If he's yours then . . . " the girl said relaxing her grip on him.

Kitty protested, "No. Lex was, at least we started off in a good way, until he got shot . . . and lost his arm and I'm to blame."

Jason protested, "No Katherine, no one is to blame. It was an attack, maybe on all three of us."

Madam Canzioni again raised her hand, "No one's to blame for this tragedy." She went on, "If you want a room with Jason we have a spare bedroom, the nicest in the house."

Kitty protested, "No! Ms. Canzioni, we're not that way."

"Call me Bella," She said and then nodded to the dark haired girl, "All right, Darilyn, you take Jason up to a bedroom and--" she shook her finger at her, "--make sure he gets a night's sleep, understand. You take it easy on him!?" Darilyn nodded and took Jason's arm leading him to the stairway. Kitty could see she was smiling along the way. For that matter so was Jason and she guessed Ella was becoming only a distant memory.

"And Katherine," I have a room for you. You can relax and put your thoughts in order. Tomorrow we will have a plan. I'm sure," she looked from Kitty to Jason, " it will all be better tomorrow."

For some reason Madam Canzioni's optimism was rubbing off on Kitty and she was starting to feel better and if Carg leaves her alone it will be a better night.

Chapter Thirteen

Everyone at the Port of Entry heard about the shooting and of Lex's wound. Adams was advised by the medical staff that a new mechanical arm was already under construction for Lex. It would take a few weeks to attach once the swelling in Lex's arm went down but it would cost a fortune which Lex didn't have. Adams felt that his company, Aztec Lines, should have covered the cost of his arm but they squawked about Lex not strictly being on company business while he was walking out of the Port of Entry. Money grubbing buzzards, he thought.

"Captain!" Mira called as she carried the last of her personal belongings off the Escadril. She had resigned her 'Pleasure Pal' position with Aztec and was planning a new Venture in Europa's largest city, Ilandia. "You seem more morose than usual."

"I have to apologize for not being the positive, happy leader of our family." Adams always referred to his crew as a family and to him it was the closest he had since the accident.

"I guess you've heard what happened to Lex yesterday," she said.

"This is serious, I don't know who those assassins were after," Adams said as he stumbled and then regained his stance, " but when I got Jason and the other women off Luna they became my responsibility and this shooting is a total mystery. Why would anyone? Was it Katherine they were after or Jason...it could have been either one. And then Lex gets his arm blown off."

"Captain, Lex's been one of my best friends for almost three years now, I've got a bundle saved, I can pay for his arm..." Mira said as she pulled out a bank transfer disk. She didn't say anything, but she had noticed the apparent weakness in the Captain. It seemed to be something progressive.

"Mira, that's generous of you but no, I'll pay for it. But from what I heard from Lex, he wasn't the target. It was either Jason or Katherine. Why would they be after either one of them? Jason? For desertion?"

"Or after Katherine," Mira added. "You know why she was sent up in the first place."

"Yes, but can those people think she's still a threat to them. I mean we're a half billion miles from that rebellion."

Mira frowned, "Yes but revolutions spread. And I think that's one of the crimes that Europa and Earth consider too dangerous to forgive. Governments are funny that way." She paused for a few seconds, "I gave Katherine an address of a friend of mine here in the city. She might be there and she may know something by now."

"Good, please check that out. You have my ID contact. I want to know what you find. Especially where Jason is, he was part of that shootout...he must be feeling terrible, the poor kid."

****

Already down to the breakfast room of Madam Canzioni's, Kitty looked up the stairwell to the first level and saw Jason and Darylyn emerge from one of the rooms. She was buttoning up a slightly more wrinkled version of what she was barely wearing last night, and Jason, with a distinctly red face, emerged tucking his shirt inside his pants. She kissed him on the cheek and walked away probably to her own room. He is certainly handling the shoot out better than Kitty, she had barely gotten any sleep and repeatedly saw the flash of the stunner blowing off Lex's arm. Only now it was in slow motion. Maybe Jason's military training helped him retain a sense of balance after that violent act and an evening with that girl didn't hurt.

Darylyn had already left for unknown parts of the upstairs and Jason was starting down the stairs. He had a slight grin on his face, this young man who just two days before had pleaded with Kitty for advice on how to deal with Ella dumping him. Did he even remember who Ella was?

Madam Canzioni emerged from the kitchen area and sat across the breakfast table from Kitty. Looking up at Jason descending the stairs and Darylyn's retreat to her room, she shook her head.

"I told that girl to take it easy on the boy. He went through such an ordeal and look at him. He has to hold on to the rail to keep from falling down the stairs. She never listens."

Following Jason down the stairs and passing him half way down was Tianne. She was wearing a see-through robe and Jason was making a concerted effort, looking off to the side and up at the ceiling, not to stare at her but, of course, he did.

"Tianne, would you put something on, we have company." Canzioni complained.

The girl looked at herself and frowned. Then she reached in a pocket, retrieved a small device, tweaked it and her robe started to darken until it was totally opaque.

"I'm sorry, I forget sometimes how to live in a normal world...is this better?" she said continuing down the stairs.

Kitty had seen this kind of clothing transducer before but was surprised that the fashion had already gotten to Ilandia. It came in handy when you had only one or two outfits, changing colors expanded your options. It was an expensive fashion but the girls here probable could afford those things. Madam Canzioni's seemed like a very expensive house.

"Much better," Madam Canzioni said motioning to the table, "come on join us."

Jason also approached and Kitty noticed that he glanced one or two times at Tianne's outfit. He probably preferred the transparent version.

Jason mumbled something about a cup of coffee and Tianne who was already at the dispenser prepared him a cup.

Kitty looked at Jason who seemed to be trying to widen his eyes.

"Jason, do you need toothpicks to keep your eyes open, you can't really go back to sleep," she said, but realized that maybe he didn't get that much sleep if he was with Darylyn. "We have to do something today," she said.

Jason looked at her and after a second, which was the time it took for her remark to register, said,

"What...what do we have to do? Hide? Where?" He paused to sip his drink, "I was thinking that those assassins somehow knew we were on that ship and then on that shuttle. Only the crew knew that."

Kitty's eyes widened when she realized what he was saying, "It was one of the crew who must have contacted someone here in Ilandia. But were they after you or me?"

Tianne, who was seated across from Kitty, perked up and said, "I think it was you," and she motioned to Kitty. Every one turned to face Tianne waiting for an explanation. She continued sipping her coffee.

"Well?" an expectant Madam Canzioni said.

"Well, I had a customer last. A really rich guy, connected . . . " and she sipped her coffee again.

"And?" Canzioni prompted again.

"Well, after we played around, you know."

Finally Madam Canzioni slammed her hand on the table, "Child! Don't give us details about your work. How do you know it was Miss DeLumiere they were after?"

A startled Tianne spoke up, "Well, he was bragging about a contract that he was working on that was paying almost a hundred thousand credits for someone to off. . . " and she opened her free hand and indicated Kitty. "They want to get rid of her, you, because you're a threat to the government here on Europa. I'm not kidding, that's what he said and when I heard what happened. Well," She placed her coffee cup on the table, "they almost collected."

Madam Canzioni let out a puff of air, "A hundred thousand credits. Girl," she nodded towards Kitty, "they'll try again. You are valuable property. You've got to somehow stay hidden. I know enough about the city and how things are done that you can feel safe here for as long as you want to stay."

When she said that Kitty felt a great weight lifted from her. Here was someone who could help. Mira was right.

At that moment the entry signal sounded and Jason and Kitty whirled around.

"Relax children," Madam Canzioni said after glancing at her entry vid. "It's Mira and another girl. That kind of adrenaline rush can kill you. Relax, you're safe . . . for now."

Chapter Fourteen

While Kitty had only known Mira and Ella for less than a week, they were a breath of fresh air when they entered Madam Canzioni's house. They were welcomed to the breakfast table and Canzioni introduced them to the girl Tianna and then called up to the girls on the upper floor to meet the new co-owner of the house. Five girls finally showed up, most just waking up. Kitty realized this was the work that Mira had been talking about, at least for her, a relatively secure and safe future, certainly if she were to be part owner of this business. The demand for these girls wouldn't end any time soon but Kitty felt that she couldn't convince herself that Mira's life was what she wanted. Ella had chosen that path, not Kitty, even though Carg urged her to go in that direction.

Ella seemed excited about her new line of work.

"I can't believe I'm going to get paid for this," Ella said. It was something new for her. "They pay me to have fun."

Madam Canzioni asked the other girls to show Ella the ropes, get her some attractive clothes and let her settle in, be one of them, what kind of men she could expect, and what they expect. Kitty didn't quite understand her excitement, but she knew Ella was an independent spirit. Murder in her background was ignored by the Europan authorities, not so for revolutionaries. The murder of her two boyfriends also gave her some status with the other girls in the Canzioni house. They wanted to hear all about it. Details and all.

On the other hand, Kitty's life was a mess and she would always be looking over her shoulder for the police or the next assassin. The only way out would be to find a surgeon who would remove this neck transponder that she had implanted at that Lunar prison. It always gave her away and the assassins knew it and had used it. Madam Canzioni had those kinds of connections but could she stay hidden until medical help arrived. Maybe days, maybe weeks. Once free of that contraption she could change identity and really be free, especially here on Europa. Still, real freedom would only be if she could be cleared of those charges against her.

There didn't appear to be any adverse side effect of that piece of nanoscale scrap in her head unless you call Carg a side effect. In some ways it was good to have this alter ego around. She hadn't heard from her in a while and rather missed her irritating comments. They seemed to be something Kitty needed to hear.

Mira leaned closer to Kitty, "Katherine, I think Ella will be happy here, but you have been through an ordeal," she said. "Who were those gunmen after?"

Kitty looked at Tianne and then Jason, "Me," she said. "Me, I think. Why I don't know. But me! Instead they shot Lex. There seems to be a reward for me, dead or alive... those assassins were trying for dead."

"I know. I think half the city knows." Mira said sitting down at their table. She continued, "The governor of Europa is furious and wants an all-out investigation but the news reports are already talking about you, Kitty, as the one who shot the two men. They're framing you as the gun happy trouble maker, the rebel and no government likes rebels. They say Lex got hurt when the men were trying to defend themselves and that they fired in self-defense."

When she heard this Kitty's mouth dropped open, "What! What! " Again in disbelief.

"Lex can tell them what happened. They have to ask him," she protested.

"They can't. Lex is in the hospital under sedation."

"But I saw what happened." Jason blurted out. "I can tell them what happened."

"No you can't Jason," Kitty said raising her arm as if to say 'stop'. "You have enough to worry about. Remember they want you too. And they wouldn't believe you anyway. You deserted, show your head and they'll throw you in prison or send you back to the Centauri system. No. Mira, Tianne here," Kitty motioned to Tianne sitting at their table, "has inside information that they want me. I've got a price on my head, a hundred thousand credits."

Mira had raised eyebrows on hearing of the money being offered for Kitty, "They must really believe that you are a threat to the government here. That must be the reason, Wow!"

"Kitty, I've been listening to what's going on and there's only one way out." It was Carg again. *"Just tell the police the truth and that should explain it all. You should feel good, a hundred thousand credits is a lot of money."*

It was good to her from her alter ego. Kitty held a straight face but smiled internally. *"Carg, maybe truth works on your world but that's not how it works here."*

In fact truth did work on the planet Mondara. Hand held lie detectors were easily available and no-one dared lie..at least outright lies.

"Well, then Lex, your boyfriend, should be able to tell them when he wakes up."

"Carg, that could be a long..." before she could finish the thought to Carg, it dawned on Kitty that if there was a contract on her for so much money and they wanted to frame her for the killings then Lex might be in danger. He was in the hospital, knocked out with drugs, who knows what they might do to him to keep him from telling exactly what happened. Maybe they don't want the truth out. Maybe the assassins were hired by the governor or even someone higher up.

Madam Canzioni muttered a few "tsk, tsks" and said, "Children!" Apparently she thought of them all as her wards, "We will hide you until we can locate a surgeon to remove that contraption you have. What is it a transponder? Then you can find a little peace and maybe come work for us."

"There," Carg said to Kitty, *"She has a solution and this would be the perfect place to study anthropology."*

Kitty ignored Carg and looked from Mira to Madam Canzioni, "I just had a frightening thought. What if Lex is in danger at the hospital. Could it be that someone doesn't want the truth to get out, that those guys shot at me first."

Madam Canzioni stared at Kitty. "Katherine, you have a mind like my own. Of course! I should have thought of that. This all sounds like something the mayor would concoct if his buttocks were on the line. I know him. He's got orders from higher up." She thought for another few seconds and turned towards Mira, "It is very likely a dangerous situation for your friend," she said; then patted Kitty's arm, "Child, I have several customers, medical students and a few doctors that wouldn't want their wives to know what they do in their spare time and they owe me favors. I will see if they can do something."

"But I should help, I got him into this trouble," Kitty said.

Mira was shaking her head ,

"Katherine, you don't know your way around Ilandia, let alone the hospital, you're hot property." Mira nodded to Madam Canzioni, "Bella knows the best chance of getting to Lex is her way. Medical students, doctors, who know their way around the Wards. Excuse me," she said as her wrist vid signaled. She moved to the side of the room to answer it and then looked back at Kitty.

"Katherine, it's Sadoka. She's worried about the Captain," Mira said to the image. Kitty rose and went next to Mira where she could see the image of Sadoka. "Tell Katherine what you told me."

"Katherine, the Captain has contracted for an ice trawler and, from what I can tell he's going to search for his wife's body. He thinks he has the right coordinates. It's some place several hundred miles from here. He's going to kill himself looking for her. It's cold out there and he can barely get around."

Kitty looked over to Jason who apparently overheard the conversation and was already heading in Mira's direction.

"Wait, Sadoka. He'll never find her." Jason said, "It's crazy. She could be down any one of the crevasses. There were a hundred of them. I searched."

"Jason, you tell him that. It won't do any good. I think he's obsessed with finding her," Kitty shouted.

Sadoka seemed almost beside herself, at one point biting her fingernail. "I'm going to go with him, he needs someone to help run that trawler, keep him from killing himself."

Jason frowned, looked over to Kitty, then looked up to see Darilyn standing on the second floor balcony. Then to Mira and Sadoka, "Tell the Captain, I'm going too." Darilyn set her lips and turned and walked away. Jason called after her, "Darilyn, I'll be back in less than a week." She didn't look back. "Wait for me," he added. She turned and looked at him and mouthed the words-'four days'. Then she said, "I'll wait."

Kitty looked over to Jason, "You're not leaving me. I'm going too. I can't stay here. I'd just sit here and worry and if they ever found I was here, Madam Canzioni would be in big trouble. But I can't do anything on a ship." She thought for a few seconds, "except be a cook, but I'm going. I'd be a mental blob if the Captain hadn't rescued me from that Lunar asylum. Or worse, I'd be in the Venus prison system. I'm going with you."

Past indiscretions were ignored as long as present behavior fit in with what was considered proper. This attitude seemed to suit the Europan society as long as certain activities remained under the radar. Revolutionaries were a different matter since their target was the government itself. Madam Canzioni's business was one of those activities that was ignored as long as decorum was maintained, but she was well aware of the need of her customers to make a discrete exit from her establishment since so many preferred to hide from curious eyes. Kitty and Jason were led to an exit hidden behind an easily moveable partition in the lower level of her house. Mira had arranged
or an air car to take them back to the shipping section of the Ilandia Port.

Both Kitty and Jason were grateful that there were no ID scans as you entered the Port from the more industrial side of the city. They found Sadoka already at the ship manifest counter and found her fears were correct.

"Here," Sadoka said pointing to the manifest posted on the vid-screen, "an Ice Trawler was contracted for by a Captain Brace Adams."

Kitty looked at the listing and followed it to the last column, "It's scheduled to leave in 35 minutes! Terminal five. We don't even have an hour."

"Come on! Back to the car!" Jason shouted as he took Kitty's arm, "This port is big and we need to get to that terminal and it's down the other side."

The three raced back to the air car and found that the driver was more than willing to speed down the landing port areas dodging sky-lifts, fork lifts carriers and the occasional innocent bystander or stevedore. After Terminal four they stopped in confoundment. There was no terminal five. No five! Looking around Kitty noticed a tunnel just before the ice wall.

"That's gotta be it," she said breathlessly.

"There's nothing else, let's go." Jason shouted and led them back to the waiting air car. In spite of his dislike for the military Jason had that take control attitude which Kitty admired.

Just outside the tunnel the driver stopped. "I can't go in there," he said, there are ID checks and permits.

The three jumped out and saw that a dimly lit sign half way up the tunnel did read, 'Terminal Five' and several hundred meters ahead of that was parked an Ice Trawler with its spiked tracks, its driving lights flashing and its rear entry door, still open but slowly closing.

"What is all this excitement, Katherine? Your adrenaline is really running high." In the mad rush to get to Captain Adams, Kitty had forgotten about Carg.

"Carg, can you get to Captain Adams and tell him to wait for us?" Kitty thought as she and the others were running and occasionally shouting at Adams amidst catching breaths. Adrenaline Levels! It made sense that if Carg was a creature locked in Kitty's brain that she might be sensitive to Kitty's various hormone levels. No wonder she's so interested in my love life.

"No Hun, I only talk to you, sorry," was Carg's answer.

The entry gangway to the trawler was almost closed with only a small crack of light coming through when it stopped, paused and then reversed itself and opened. The stairway unfolded and down came the familiar figure of Captain Adams accompanied by Cody Williams, the Escadril's communications officer.

Chapter Fifteen

Now was not the time to remain in Ilandia. If Kitty returned in perhaps in a week or two, things might have cooled off and maybe Madam Canzioni could find a surgeon to get that thing out of her neck. They called it a transponder but it was really a chain around her neck and it might as well be choking her. It had also been her goal to remove the nanoscale brain implant but conversations with Carg were helping her gain an insight into her own personality and if Carg was responsible for the new algorithms speeding up the ship maybe her advanced world could help in some way. The only side effect was Carg's sarcastic nature.

Kitty was sorting through a selection of thermal suits from the terminal's collection. They had miniature Snap Generators in each one providing electricity for heating and an appropriate pressure gradient throughout the suit for at least several weeks of exposure to upside conditions. Wearing a suit was essential for anyone going to the surface

"Katherine, I can understand the Captain wanting to put...how do you say...closure to his wife's fate."

"Carg, sometimes you can be understanding," Kitty said mentally, then added, *"with other people's problems. You never sympathize with any of my problems. Why is that?"*

In Kitty's mind view Carg was now standing at the bottom level of the boarding gangway leading up to the Trawler. She was already wearing one of the thermal outfits that Kitty had just inspected. It was of a glistening black fabric and it fit her shape so that every curve was emphasized. Kitty quickly sorted through the suits and found one like the one Carg had and folded it over her arm. She's not going to outclass me, she thought.

"Katherine," Carg said as she proceeded up the gangway into the ship, *"My project is to study your culture and you are part of that but I can't help making suggestions when you are about to do something dumb."*

Kitty thought that 'dumb' according to Carg was Kitty simply trying to keep a little self-respect and not be the kind of Pleasure Pal Anthropologist that Carg wanted her to be. Before Kitty could answer that creature with a snappy come back, Sadoka touched her arm.

"Look," Sadoka said and pointed to an air taxi that had just arrived where two men dressed as hospital orderlies were helping Lex maneuver out onto the terminal entry. Both Kitty and Sadoka rushed over and realized Lex, heavily bandaged, was still incoherent, very likely drugged at the hospital. They took Lex's limp body from the men who quickly excused themselves saying,

"Captain Adams' crew?" Sadoka nodded, saying "Yes, but..."

The orderly helped Kitty take Lex's good arm, "Here, you've got him, he's yours now. We weren't here! You never saw us," he said and rapidly made his way back to the taxi which vanished down the concourse. This had to be the work of Madam Canzioni. She said she could get Lex out of the Hospital and she did it in a matter of an hour. That kind of influence is remarkable Kitty thought.

She and Sadoka , with Jason's help, managed to get Lex up the gangway, into the Trawler and into sleeping quarters. He seemed so loaded with sedatives and pain killers that he was unaware of what was happening but if Canzioni's and Kitty's suspicions were correct they had saved Lex's life.

With all aboard the trawler, and the gangway locked to the trawler, the Captain, in communication with Terminal Control, gave the order to begin the ascent to the surface. They proceeded to the open Door No.1 and, chugging along, they reached the ice surface   in about 30 minutes. They had gone six miles climbing steadily through the access tunnel carved mostly from ice which here was slightly more than a mile thick. The tunnel was brightly lit but on reaching the surface the lights powered by Ilandia generators ended and they were faced with the dim frozen landscape of Europa, Ice and more ice as far as anyone could see. Kitty gawked at the last thermometer which read forty degrees. Kitty turned to Jason who was donning his thermal suit. "Forty degrees, that's not too bad," she said.

He turned to her, "Katherine, they switched, that's the Kelvin Scale, it's really four hundred below zero outside, that's if you want to use Fahrenheit. When he said that a chill ran down her spine and she thought of times in the Eritrean desert, basking in the warm sun.

Days before when they arrived at Europa, the shuttle took her down to Ilandia. They were going from cold to a comfortable warm city. This way was different. She thought of the stories about the heat on the planet Venus and how a prison sentence on Venus might have been the better option. Which would she prefer, to be frozen solid or burned to a crisp.

"Katherine!" Carg appeared dressed now in a light springtime outfit. *"Get those morbid thoughts out of your head. So far, under the circumstances, I think you've done the right things. I might have preferred you working at Madam Canzioni's but I understand your respect thing. I just think it's a luxury you can't afford. Girl, you are getting in deeper and deeper. But, on the other hand, my research is looking better and better."*

Kitty's conversation with Carg was interrupted by the Captain who wanted a meeting with his so-called crew. They gathered at the bridge command center where the Captain looked them over and said,

"You people are something. What did you think I was going to do, run out on the ice and freeze my nose on the iceberg with Laura in it, that is if I ever found her?"

"Captain," Sadoka said, "We know how you felt about your wife, can you blame us. We didn't know how far you were going to go up here on the ice. And you were going out alone. That's scary. You've pulled us out of some tight situations and I, myself, owe you a lot...my whole career for one thing."

Cody joined in, "Me too, Captain. I was right out of Space academy and you took me on. I didn't want to see you make a . . . "

Adams finished his sentence, "A mistake?" he said. "People, my goal on this trip is two-fold. Yes, I am going to look for Laura's body but I have no desire to commit suicide, my myolitus will take care of that. I have the reports of Jason's search team and right now we are within a three hundred kilometers of the wreck site. She's got to be out there and I have to convince myself there's nothing more to do. Or maybe there is. If she's entirely in ice there's the possibility she can be revived." He then looked around the command center,

"Yes, it would have been difficult but not impossible. Most of the trawler can be put on Robotic control."

Kitty felt the Captain was grasping at the thinnest of straws. From what she knew about Jupiter, it poured out enough radiation to bake a pizza. How could Laura's body possibly survive that even if she was in a block of ice. Besides that the Captain looked more fragile than ever.

The Captain continued, "I want to spend time searching for Laura and if I can't find her or at least convince myself that it's hopeless and she's truly lost. No doubt she is frozen but where? Exposed? Encased in ice? What? I have to do my best before . . . "

Jason, silent till this time spoke up, "Captain you know the research on resuscitating frozen bodies and organs?"
Adams smiled and replied, "Yes Jason, I know, more than five years at liquid nitrogen temps give a 62 percent successful recovery and every year after that the success rate drops. That's why this trip is so important. Five years is coming up... after that the chances drop to less than 50 percent."

Chapter Sixteen

Kitty had imagined that an ice trawler would be skimming across a smooth shinny frozen lake of ice but Europa was not like that. Jupiter's radiation belt ate into the ice and made a tumbled field of mini ice bergs and deep ditches and crevasses on the surface. The ice sublimed and re-condensed into boulder like structures covered with snow. The trawlers independent wheel and track design handled it but tumbled those inside whenever they came across a large out-cropping, space sickness pills helped. Everyone complained except Lex who seemed to be sleeping through it all. He was lucid at times and Sadoka kept him alert with conversation.

Sadoka seemed to care for him and in some ways Kitty felt a tinge of jealousy. Lex had helped Kitty through the space walk and she needed someone afterwards. Was that all it was? She wondered if it was possible for her to have a serious relationship with anyone any more. Lex was great but was it only a fleeting comfort? And really, how did he feel after losing an arm protecting Kitty.

"Kitty, you are fine .From our study of human psychology, you need a more stable environment. You'll be fine once these troubles you've brought upon yourself are resolved."

Carg had once again tried to be helpful but only succeeded in irritating Kitty.

"Carg, my only mistake was trusting Orlando the Rat and..." as she thought this it dawned on her that Carg was right. Until she

could put her feelings for or against Orlando to rest she might not ever be able to trust a man again. Now it was obvious. *"You are right. But it's not easy."*

Sitting in front of the Vid screen showing the ice flows they were making their way across, Kitty reflected on Carg's obvious truth but soon was interrupted as Jason approached. He sat next to her. "You must think I'm an idiot," he said. Kitty was surprised.

"Jason, I don't think you're an idiot, what're you talking about? You saved my life. You're my hero."

"Maybe not an idiot, maybe fickle, but here I am only two days after leaving Ella and I'm involved with Darylyn." He sighed. "I thought Ella was it and now everything has changed."

"Jason, you know Ella is more of a free spirit. She didn't want to be tied down with. . ."

Jason finished her sentence, "a husband, I know, with kids."

Kitty continued, "Right now that's how she feels. You have to move on and if you and Darylyn hit it off, good. Find out what she wants, if it's what you want it's even better."

Carg suddenly appeared to Kitty, she was still dressed in her black skin tight outfit.

"Katherine, that's very sensible advice. I didn't think you were capable of that. Now you should follow it yourself." Of course, another insult from Carg, Kitty thought. Carg continued, *"Forget Orlando, accept things as they are. He's gone. Move on. Orlando was just a part of your life's learning process."*

"Carg, for once you're being sensible."

"Thank you, Katherine, but I know you and I look forward to more emotional turmoil that gets you into trouble. I really am grateful to you."

Kitty was taken aback by that, *"Why grateful?"* she thought back.

"Katherine, my group leaders on my world are fascinated by what's happening to you and they want to keep funding this

connection just to see how your life winds up. Some even have bets on how long you'll live."

"That's terrible, Carg. That's disgusting."

"No it's not. I'm betting you'll survive." Saying that, Carg vanished.

Jason looked at Kitty, "Katherine, you looked like you were daydreaming. Maybe we shouldn't talk about my personal problems."

Kitty smiled, "Jason, that's not it. I have a lot running around in my head."

"Yes. Ella told me," he said in all seriousness, "Your spiritual advisor."

Ella did say that and maybe she was right. But why did my spiritual advisor have to be so irritating and right at the same time. Katherine debated about telling Jason that Carg claimed to be from a different world and all the other details, but decided spiritual advisor was as good as any other explanation.

"I sometimes wish I had a spiritual advisor." Jason said, "Maybe it would help me deal with women."

Kitty smiled. She felt Jason was doing just fine. He was young, that's all. Maybe her role as 'the older woman' had helped, but Ella would be a challenge to any man. And who knows about Darylyn, especially after working at Madam Canzioni's.

Kitty thought about the comfort the girls at Canzioni's were living in. She envied that. Right now she was feeling cold just looking at the Vid Screen of the ice world in front of them; ice bergs tens of meters high off to their right side and kilometers across, they were traversing a flat lake of ice with crisscrossing crevasses off to their left side, some so deep they couldn't see their bottom as the trawler scooted by. Each time the trawler's lights would scan the horizon and they could see their path ahead through the frozen debris. Most of the time their path was smooth but at times there was no progress forward unless they climbed over boulders of ice blocking their way. The captain knew his way through this ice world even though there was no doubt he hated it. It's possible he could have made this trip without help but she felt better knowing there were more than just robotic eyes involved in a trek across this frozen wasteland.

****

"Captain," Williams called out to him, "we are at the co-ordinates of the accident and I'm scanning for any debris. So far nothing."

Captain Adams wheeled his chair over to Williams and the two of them searched the videos of the ice scene. Their flood-lights revealed a wide expanse of flat ice crisscrossed by crevices, some no more than a meter deep but at times cut by a wide crevasse.

"I'm scanning each of the crevasses with penetrating radar but again nothing, but I can't see down to their bottom."

Adams was intent on the video image and on the radar signal which was projected on the screen. It was mostly a flat line with minor ups and downs, indicating ice and nothing more. They could see the change from ice to atmosphere in the shallower crevasses clearly but nothing like the mass of a human body which would have easily been picked up as a sharp deviation of the signal. They made the usual spiral search pattern round and round in ever widening circles but found nothing remarkable.

Sadoka knew that the search was a disappointing effort for the Captain as he seemed to sink back in his chair, and be more and more restless.

"I'm expanding the pattern to a two kilometer area," Sadoka said although she knew that this search was increasingly frustrating. Chances of finding the body were slim. "It's possible that the co-ordinates are off since Jupiter's radiation levels are constantly changing. Those location coordinates are really sensitive to small changes . They don't have a reliable GPS system in place yet. And I can't probe the deeper crevasses."

Adams backed his chair away from the screen. "I have to see for myself," he said. "I'll take the radar probe and check the deep ones. That's where she is. I feel it." He got up from his chair and made his way, haltingly to the side cabinet and pulled out an environment suit.

Kitty looked over to Sadoka and Williams who seemed concerned looking at the Captain struggling with the suit. Sadoka finally said, "Captain, you can't..."

He interrupted her, "I have to, she's out there. At the bottom."

Jason stepped over to the Captain and helped him with the suit but Sadoka raised her hand as if to say 'stop'. "Captain! I'm not letting you go out there. Sit down! You are in no condition to be climbing over the ice fields," she said in a voice Kitty had never heard before. Jason looked at the Captain who for an instant seemed to protest but sagged into Jason's arms.

"Captain," Jason said, "I'll go out there. I've had training in this kind of work. Remember. I was a junior Ice Ranger." He helped Adams back to his chair and took the suit from him.

Sadoka paused for a second, "Jason, you're not going out there without a partner."

Lex lifted his head and volunteered, "I'll go," he said. Kitty and everyone else knew Lex was barely able to stand and it was really a just reflex of the kind of man he was.

Kitty rose from her chair, "Jason, I agree, you've got to have a partner out there. It cannot be Lex or the Captain. Both of you have to get your strength back. Sadoka has to drive the trawler over the ice, I just don't trust AI for what we're doing; we could all wind up over a cliff and Cody," she nodded to him, "we need you to interpret the radar. That leaves me."

Chapter Seventeen

Did she actually say she was going out there? Kitty stood there staring at the others, Sadoka, Cody, the Captain and Jason. She remembers the words and gave a quick thought to blaming Carg for that out-burst, but no, Carg had nothing to do with it. It was Kitty's own sense of fairness that erupted. That's the problem. When you have not been treated fairly yourself, you develop an acute sense of what is fair.

Jason, now almost dressed in his enviro-suit looked at her, "Of course, Katherine, that makes sense. It will not be too bad. Lots of girls are in the Ice Rangers. You can do it," he said as he zipped up the suit and twisted on his helmet. "I think all you have to do is follow me as my backup. If something happens you can help and visa-versa. It's always a good idea to have two on the ice. Besides we can only stay out for a few hours. Too much radiation."

Williams agreed, "Katherine, you'll be fine. We'll be in constant contact and I'll give you both the radar findings. If we find something we can proceed from there. But you can't be out too long."

Sadoka looked over to the Captain who seemed to be deep in thought. "Captain, if Laura's out there we'll find her," she said. "We can expand the search spiral another kilometer and there are several deep trenches we can look at. Jason will have the probe and I think its capability is a 100 meter depth. We'll find her."

"Thank you all," Adams said. "You know I appreciate all of this. But I know you all are thinking this is a fool's errand. She's gone. It's been five years. I don't want you risking your lives over this." He had the sound of someone having given up.

Kitty, with her suit half-way on struggled to the Captain and, putting her hand on his shoulder said, "It doesn't matter Captain. We will search until we can't anymore. Let me repay you. I have to."

In a matter of minutes Jason hoisted up the backpack for the radar probe and was ready to go. Kitty had her suit on, helmet in place and followed him out the airlock onto the dim ice-scape. Looking up she was startled. This was the first time she was standing on a solid floor, not terra-firma but ice-a firma, looking up at the sky. The last time was on earth, but now she saw many more stars all against an almost black sky, and then the bright disk of Jupiter filling half the sky. She stood there for several seconds entranced until Jason nudged her to follow him.

"Let's get a look at the channel up ahead," and he pointed to a dark streak several meters up the ice slope they were standing on.

Jason marched ahead digging his cramp-ons into the ice and making his way up the steep slope to the edge of the crevasse that Williams had already looked at it using the ship's probe but saw nothing. Kitty followed digging the hard spikes of her boots into the ice and crunching her way up to his side.

"How do you do this?" She asked watching him kneel by the edge.

"It's simple. I wave the wand slowly from side to side and Williams can reconstruct what's down there almost a hundred meters into the ice below. It's like a sonogram."

She heard Williams through her sound system, "Nothing, Jason, it seems all uniform. Ice and more ice."

Jason then slowly made his way up the slope to another crack not much more than a meter wide, stepped across it and went farther up the ice to another and repeated the wand scan. It went like this for almost two hours and Williams reported nothing special. Crossing back to the other side of the main crevasse, Jason with Kitty following him, started down to another channel almost a hundred meters away. Again he knelt and waved the radar wand. Williams reported nothing new. Jason moved on another thirty meters and Williams voice came through loud and clear." There, something... It's vague ."

On the Trawler, Williams glued himself to the video reconstruction which slowly improved in resolution as Jason repeatedly scanned. "It's something man made, sharp angular corners, possible metallic," he said. The excitement of finding something was dulled by William's description that it was not Laura, not a human body. Yet finding something in this forsaken frozen world was special.

Amidst the murmuring of Sadoka and Adams, Lex announced that he recognized what it was a part of the stability module of a ship much like the 'Escadril'. "I think it might be from the Margarita. And if this came off on your approach, Captain, you would have lost attitude control." He looked over to the Captain who also was studying the artifact image.

"If that's true some bastard mechanic didn't assemble it right back on the lunar base," Adams said turning away in disgust.

"Captain," Lex continued, "Good records are kept and we can find out who worked on it before you left. Whoever he or she is, is responsible for those deaths when the ship crashed. They have to be prevented from doing this kind of sloppy work again."

"Good, then we'll string 'em up," Adams added.

On the ice Kitty was studying her endurance gauge. "Jason, my gauge says I'm down to fifteen percent. Let's go back. The cold is starting to come through. I'm freezing."

Jason looked at her and studied his own gauge." Katherine that's fifteen percent used up, we still have 85 percent left, you can't be cold." Fortunately he had the signal to Cody blocked and was talking only with Kitty.

"Don't tell me I'm not cold. I can't feel my feet. I'm going back." She shouted although the audio connection was working perfectly, he almost could hear her without any connection.

"All right, all right! We go back." Saying that, he turned towards the ship digging in his cramp-ons heading towards the light of the airlock. Kitty led the way. He turned on the ship audio.

"Cody, nothing. So far nothing looks familiar," Jason said, as he looked over the ice-scape. "I don't remember any of the ice structures around here."

"These are the coordinates." Cody said. "But you know the ice can shift."

"By that much? Can't be. But something's not right. We'll keep looking." It was slowly getting darker and the shadows of the ice ridges were getting longer. "We're heading back. Our radiation limit is approaching. But there's another cascade up a little further, we'll go up the slope Just to check it out. By the way, pass the word, Katherine is doing well." He looked over to Kitty standing by his side, "She's with me every step of the way."

Kitty heard this and decided she needn't squash the image, but she felt cold and tired. They had been out for three hours and she swore the suit wasn't working yet the thermometer readouts measuring her body temp and inside suit temps said she was supposed to be comfortable. What does it know.

Jason started up the ice slope but their speakers activated again. It was Cody. "Jason, Katherine, head back to the ship immediately. We have a crisis in the making. We need you back here, Captain's orders."

Chapter Eighteen

Seated around the main table of the Command Center, both Jason and Kitty were surprised and got to their feet when Sadoka came in with Lex leaning on her. Lex was pale but seemed alert and smiled at those gathered. "Captain, everyone, greetings from my drugged out world and I want to thank you all for getting me out of that pit of a hospital." He nodded to Sadoka, "Thank you Sadoka, I think I can manage now." He then, by himself, made his way to one of the chairs around the table.

"Welcome, Lex I'm glad you're here." We have a decision to make and all of us should be involved. You all know my original intention was to find the body of my wife, Laura. I still intend do that but Lieutenant Cody has received some communications that may delay us." He turned to Cody who was still inputting commands into the Comm Center console, " Tell us what you've found so far."

Cody threw several switches and an image formed on the screen in back of his console.

"Yes, sir. This is what I picked up a few minutes ago," he said as the screen flickered. He entered a few more commands and there appeared a clear image of a woman seated at a ship's bridge. She was dressed in a typical Merchant Commanders uniform. In the background the interior of a ship much like the trawler they were on could be seen and a small fire was burning. Two others of the crew were attempting to fight the fire, choking on the fumes. "...been attacked. Mayday...Mayday, 'Falcon 5' calling . We are a non-military cargo trawler. Our attackers hijacked our cargo. I am including our coordinates with this message. Please help. We can last for maybe another hour. Severe leaks. We've been attacked. Mayday ..." and the message repeated itself.

"Cody continued, "I tried to contact them but couldn't. It may be too late."

Those seated at the table seemed stunned and were silent for a few seconds until Kitty looked around at the others and said, "They've been hijacked! Well, we don't have choice. We have to help. Can we help?" She looked over to the Captain who was silent. "Captain?"

"Katherine, Katherine, it's possible we can help. Their coordinates put them within thirty kilometers of here over some rough ice formations, so that means we could be there in perhaps twenty minutes. But hijackers can be dangerous people if they are still around."

Lex spoke up. "Captain, we have no weapons, that cargo trawler is like the trawler we're on. You can tell that kind of damage is from high power stunners and if they've punctured their hull it won't be long before everyone freezes or suffocates. Do we have time to get to them?"

"Yes, we're on no tight schedule. But it is risky." Adams said

Kitty realized what that meant. They couldn't risk five more lives if they couldn't defend themselves, but sitting here so close was frustrating.

Jason pulled out his hand stunner. "This still is loaded," he said, "but it's no match for what the hijackers might have. It won't penetrate any kind of armor."

The Captain limped over to a side cabinet, "It's no match but may still be useful. Here's what I have in mind. We have to decide quickly." He unlocked the storage cabinet and pulled out an odd looking rifle, one that seemed connected by a thick cable to a large back-pack. "I brought two of these along and hopefully was going to use them when I found Laura's body. I thought she would certainly be encased in ice." He hefted the rifle to his shoulder. "Nothing is activated yet, but when it is, the pack contains a small fusion generator using ice or water and it generates a high powered hydrogen and oxygen stream. The Europans use it to cut great swaths through the ice. That's how most of the cities were carved out. When it's on and you pull the trigger, a stream of gas or plasma is ignited and at 5000 degrees it cuts through ice instantly. It vaporizes it. Anything else is turned into a plasma."

Jason stood, "Captain," he said, "You think this would work as a weapon? I've used them before when we kids drilled tunnels to the Rec center. Pretty damn dangerous if you don't take care. One kid almost lost a hand."

"Well, Jason, of course they're dangerous, but if we do encounter these ice hijackers, I think these could be very effective. But only if we can surprise them. With their power stunners they could destroy us so we have to get to them first."

Kitty raised her hand, "Captain, I say we help. You all have helped me. I just can't sit here and not try to help them." At that instant she heard Carg's voice,

"I thought you promised to think before you speak. Now look at what you're getting us into."

Lex looked up from his resting place on Sadoka's shoulder, "I'm all for it. But surprise is essential."

Adams nodded, "With the proper pressure adjustment you can get the plasma to ignite at any distance from the barrel up to a hundred meters. If we do respond we have to approach carefully. Anyone have a counter argument?" He looked over to Cody who nodded, "I say we help, Captain."

Sadoka also spoke up, "I think we have to try."

"All right! I want Jason on one of the torches, I'll take the other. We will..."

Kitty jumped up, "Captain you're not in a position of go leaping over those ice cubes out there. Excuse me but you can barely walk." She walked over to him and took the torch from him.

"It may be mutiny but I'm going. I'm still 100% fit. In fact I still have most of my earth strength left. Lex can't go, Cody has to monitor the Comm center. Just like before!" She looked over to Sadoka.

Adams added, "Sadoka's got to manually drive this tub. The AI robotic system won't take us where we might have to go. Katherine, I appreciate the gesture, but I go."

"No you don't, Captain. I go." Kitty insisted. She looked around to the others. "Vote on it, me or the Captain. Majority rule. Who's for the Captain going out there?" Kitty looked around. Sadoka shifted her weight but kept her hand down. Cody slowly raised his hand as did Lex. Nothing more, then she said, "all right, who votes for me." Kitty asked. Sadoka raised her hand as did Jason.

Carg appeared already dressed in the pressure suit Kitty had on before, but this time it was bright red,

"I vote for you too. I think you can do it. I'm impressed. My bosses are impressed too and they've given me better odds that you're going to get killed this time. You go girl and show them."

Kitty repressed a smile and then raised her own hand. "I have a vote Captain and I'm stronger than anybody here."

"Katherine, please sit down." Adams smiled. "I also have a vote and I didn't know we run a ship by majority rule, but since all our lives are on the line I just think you might be good at this, at least give us a better chance than if I go stumbling around on the ice. I agree with you. You have my vote. You will go with Jason onto the ice as we approach the hijackers."

Meanwhile Cody was entering commands into his console and announced, "Wait!" Cody interrupted. I've tri-located the Trawler and the source of the jamming signal. They're the same!"

"What!" Adams was startled. "What does that mean?" he said.

There was silence for a few seconds. Lex spoke up first,

"Captain, that could mean the hijackers are already on top of the Cargo ship. We're too late."

Adams scratched his head, "Or," He paused as he walked over to Cody's console, "it means that this is a trick and someone wants us to take the bait and go to those coordinates. But why?" He looked around, "we don't have any treasure here. Nothing of value."

Jason then raised his hand, "Yes we do." and he pointed to Kitty and all eyes followed his finger. "Someone could have found that Kitty's on this trip, on this ship. She has a price on her head of at least a hundred thousand credits."

Kitty collapsed onto the nearest chair as her friends studied her. She hung her head and then looked up.

"I'm not worth you people risking your lives, just sell me to the nearest dealer. That'll solve the problem," she said, only half joking.

Captain Adams turned to Cody, "Cody, how would they know she's on this trip? With us?"

"By now everyone knows. There's an APB on her and I'm sure the grapevine knows the price on her head. It may be that they have info from Luna about this ship leaving with possibly Kitty on board and you remember McNeil wasn't happy when he left here. He never accepted that he never found her."

Adams limped his way to his chair and sat. "Now which is it? The hijackers already on top of the cargo trawler or a trap looking to get Katherine?"

"But why not simply attack us now, right here, rather than draw us way out there." Lex asked to no one in particular and pointed with his one arm to no particular direction.

Jason moved over to Cody's console and looked over his shoulder. He pointed to a position on Cody's view screen. "Look at the topographics of that position. The coordinates they gave are right in a box canyon. Ice cliffs on three sides. If it is a trap they're waiting here." He pointed to an area on one side of the entrance to the canyon. "If we went into the canyon, they'd come around and pound us with stunners until we gave Kitty up, and then they'd probably kill the rest of us."

"No, no. Just give me up! Better, shoot me!" Kitty shouted.

110

"On the other hand," Jason went on. "If the hijackers are really attacking that cargo ship, we'd still go into the Canyon and if they're still there they could blow us off the ice. We don't have weapons. We'd have to make a U-turn or reverse course and they'd get us."

"We can't not try," Kitty said. "Let's burn them off the ice."

Chapter Nineteen

"Katherine, I'm worried about you." While Kitty knew Carg could appear at any moment it always took her by surprise when she did. This time she was dressed in a white thermal suit much like the one that Kitty was putting on again, although Kitty's was the usual dingy grey variety. How could Carg imagine something so sleek. Somehow she looked much better in it and Kitty knew her grey variety made her look pudgy. Carg was using Kitty's body image yet always looked better. How does she do that?

"You have a perverse streak. Here you are about to risk your life again and I just know you want to see me to lose my bet with my bosses."

"Carg" Kitty thought back, *"That is the dumbest thing I've ever heard. If you lose your bet, I'm dead. Not much satisfaction there."*

"I agree, and I support you but why did you vote to rescue those people?"

"That's simple, Carg, this is one of the few times in my life when I'm not at the service of some disgusting prison guard, or someone like Orlando the Rat. I'm doing something for somebody else, something I want to do. Those people need help."

"And you find satisfaction in that?"

"Yes, Carg. Finally I'm doing something I choose to do because it's the right thing. We might even save a few lives."

"Some of you humans do have that kind of altruistic streak. From my past studies throughout your history, I didn't see too much of that. A few of you stand out but not many. Just make sure I don't lose my bet. I'll be out there with you, maybe I'll see things you might miss. I've got to protect my investment. Really I'm proud of you.

"But what will you do if it's a trap? Isn't it exciting that you're a woman worth so much money."

"Yes, exciting. But I could do without the excitement. Just a nice boring life is all I want," Kitty said and her thoughts were interrupted by Jason from outside her door.

"Katherine, Sadoka has turned off the AI and were going to the coordinates Cody's found. It might be rough going. Hold on." And immediately the trawler started to heave and slew from side to side.

"Time for space sickness pills."

Carg was still there as Kitty rose up and headed for the door.

"Actually, Carg, this is exciting and I like it."

Holding on to the rails alongside of each corridor Kitty made her way following Jason to the observation area where Lex was waiting. Jason and he were both dressed in their grey thermal suits and Jason already buckled on his head visor. Kitty immediately went to Lex and helped him put his on and locked it in place. She wondered how he could function with only one arm but he would be the center gunman using Jason's stunner, that shouldn't be too troublesome. Still he had to hold on and use the stunner, but he seemed to be stable enough. Kitty and Jason would take the port and starboard sides with the fusion torches but would have to proceed ahead of the trawler on foot once they got close enough. Their opening volleys would have to be right on target and be a surprise. If they could dismantle the marauder's stunners and Jason could fire directly on them it seemed like a workable plan if only she knew how to use the fusion torch. That was next.

Cody inserted an info-cube into the console and the side screens opened to chart after chart of Trawlers equipped with a variety of weapons.

"Typical armaments," he said. "We won't know for sure what they have but we look for stunners like these." and he indicated several of the large guns and how they were mounted. He turned to Jason, "You've been around these kinds of weapons, Jason, anything special?"

Jason studied the images, "Can't tell. Very likely it's not a military vehicle, but you never know where there got their equipment. The only thing we can go on is to be prepared for any arrangement...but the torches we have are so hot they'll melt anything in their way. So we go for it. Whatever looks like a weapon. If any of it is still there."

Kitty thought that's the way a young man would think. The old phrase 'Damn the stunners, full speed ahead' seemed to be his motto. Kitty felt it might be better to be prepared first.

****

Within minutes Captain Adams announced their trawler was approaching the coordinates and while Kitty didn't know how Lex or Jason felt, she felt her own excitement building. Jason handed Lex his hand Stunner and all three exited the trawler airlock. Lex took his position in the front of the trawler while Kitty and Jason, both with fusion torches on their backs, hopped off onto again the ice . Having gone out once before she knew the feel of it and how the suit moved with her steps.

Jason gave her a quick introduction to the fusion torch and if she could keep straight what dial to turn first it might all work out. He had her check its ability on a small ice wall a few meters tall adjacent to their trawler. She dialed what Jason thought might be appropriate for a short burst and had her try it. She was startled as a blade of blue, almost colorless flame shot out almost thirty meters, cutting a swath through the ice but also three inches off their trawler's tracks as she swung the flame around. Fortunately she quickly took her finger off the trigger before too much damage was done. Over their comm system they heard the Captain,

"How's it going out there?" he said seemingly oblivious to the damage.

"Fine Captain, under control," Jason called back on their closed circuit. "Katherine had her first lesson on the torch and we're on our way over the ridge."

Kitty was grateful he hadn't mentioned what she had cut off from the trawler, the bits of iron which were now quickly sizzling, melting their way down into the ice, probably never to be seen again. Jason signaled with his hands that it was not a problem. Kitty, looking back at Lex, secure at the front of the ship with his legs wrapped about one of the support struts, noted that even through his helmet he was smiling. Was it one of those smiles that said 'See what damage girls do'. She'd show him and hefted the power unit up and the rifle torch onto her shoulder and proceeded to march alongside Jason up the escarpment of ice. Fortunately she still had earth tempered muscles and with the weak gravity of Europa, carrying her pack was not a problem.

Those damn tidal forces of Jupiter kept the pressure on the Europa ice crust and the escarpment she had her feet planted on was growing and then collapsing. They all were. That's all she needed now was the mountain of ice she was on to slither back into the kilometer thick layer of ice she had just left, or worse slide into a submerged ocean. She'd be buried like Laura. Lex had said it was unlikely since it might take a few thousand years for that to happen ... yet ... she could feel a rumbling through her suit. It wasn't her stomach, it was the ice or was she feeling the vibrations of the stunner cannons firing. If that was the case there couldn't be much left of that cargo ship. They had to get there in the next few minutes to stop this attack. She and Jason continued upward. Another hundred meters and they could see what was going on below. Jason motioned to Kitty to stay put near the top of the ridge where she would be about 30 meters from the action below. He then indicated he would climb down to get a closer attack angle.

"Fire at any of the stunners on the hijackers when I start firing," he said to Kitty. "Captain," he had connected into the ships comm system, "Begin your approach and Lex, start firing when you see the first torch ignite. And he slithered off the ridge down the other side.

"Katherine , he's as crazy as you are." It was Carg again.

"Yes, I know Carg. It's to get a better attack angle." Kitty thought that to Carg as she hefted the Fusion torch up again to her shoulder and climbed the last few feet to the edge of the cliff. She cautiously looked over the edge and saw ice and then to the far end of the valley ... more ice ... everywhere, ice but no hijacker or any Falcon. A trap! It had to be a trap. She clicked on her comm link to Jason and the Captain.

"It's a trap. There's no one here that I can see. Nothing but ice in this entire valley. Jason, it's a trap."

"I'm going to the far edge. We'll get the bastards if they're here." Jason growled over the link.

"Be careful!" Kitty whispered.

"They have to be somewhere," he said and then she heard the click of him leaving the comm link.

Kitty looked back to see the Escalante entering the Valley with Lex at the front bow holding his stunner with his one good hand.

"Captain," she yelled, "what's going on? Where is everybody?" Then to her horror she saw a trawler turn from behind one of the glacier walls and follow the Escalante into the Valley. Much like on Cody's charts it had a collection of stunners mounted on top, all aimed at their trawler. It positioned itself directly in back of the Escalante. The trap was sprung!

"It was a trap! The hijackers! They tricked us! It was a trap! Jason be careful!" She shouted.

The hijacker ship approached and fired one of its top mounted stunners and hit the rear cargo area of the Escalante, flames burst out. To her dismay she realized there was no place for the Escalante to go, it was truly a box canyon of ice. Sheer ice walls on all three sides.

Then from her comm link she heard, "Captain Adams, you are trapped. I would suggest you listen to our terms and you may go free."

Whoever the hijackers were they wanted something. Then silence for a few seconds.

Adams answered, "You bastards! What do you want?"

"We know you are traveling with a Katherine DeLumiere. Turn her over to us and we will leave you in peace. I remind you that there is no way out, you are trapped. Give us the girl and we go. Give her an insulated suit and we will retrieve her. You and your crew will be allowed to go."

Kitty felt her heart sink She called back to Adams, "Captain, I'm not worth it, just trade me to whoever they are. You can't risk your lives just because of me." She had used the closed circuit link to the bridge of the Escalante.

"Katherine," it was Adams, "They won't let any of us escape. We'll figure something else out. You stay put. And Jason?"

Kitty forgot about Jason, he was somewhere down near the bottom of both trawlers.

She called to her alter ego, *"Carg, did you hear what they want? They want me! Do you see Jason?"*

"Of course, everybody wants Katherine," she said.

Kitty could see Carg looking over the canyon below. She was using Kitty's eyes but somehow saw more than Kitty could.

"Yes, I see him but so do the hijackers! See the top stunner is turning towards him."

Carg had seen that motion and Kitty had not. Here she was using Kitty's own visual system and had noticed things she had not.

117

But should she fire first, warn Jason or what? He said wait for his first shot. Then the hijackers' turret stunner let out a stunner blast towards Jason and a huge cloud of ice mist rose up. She could not see Jason at all. They shot him! In a fury Kitty pressed the trigger on her fusion torch and the beam shot out to the hijacker ship hitting it with the hottest part of the flame. She raked it over its surface as sparks flew and then left it on as it chopped their top stunners into pieces, white hot chunks of metal flying out into the ice fields. It melted the top turret, and began burning off pieces of the exterior shielding. They must have tried to fire the stunner but with the barrel melted shut the entire rig exploded. She then concentrated the flame on the smaller stunners and they sagged and turned into small puddles of steel burning their way into the ice.

"I'll cut the bastards into pieces" she yelled as more and more of the hijackers' ship gave way to the torch.

As she said that Lex began firing his stunner and then from the side she could see Jason's torch beam begin strafing the armaments along the hijackers' side. He was alive.

"Katherine, you'd better stop or all the hijackers will be killed. Is that what you want?"

Carg had appeared and seemed horrified. Kitty took her finger off the trigger and realized she indeed was intent on killing them all. But Jason was alive. Was that him?

"Katherine," It was Jason, "Stop firing, Stop! They're taking their escape shuttle, they're leaving."

Kitty looked over the scene below and it was true, the hijackers were leaving. Their ship was mangled , unable to fire their weapons and a small shuttle retreated into the darkness.

"Jason! What happened, I thought they hit you."

"No, it hit way ahead of me and raised so much snow and ice I could get up close into a good position. You really tore them apart. Fantastic!"

Carg was sitting on the ice next to her, her hands folded over her knees.

"See, even you have that nasty human streak to lash out at someone in the heat of the moment. That was interesting."

Kitty lay there with her fusion torch off to her side. Carg had it right. She was furious with those hijackers but maybe what she was doing was venting anger at Orlando the Rat and her whole life since then. It was time to re-assess.

"Thank you Carg," She said as she looked down the ice to the Escalante and what was left of the hijacker's trawler. *"You are right, I'm one of those faulty humans."*

Chapter Twenty

Kitty lay there against the ice of the escarpment looking over the edge watching the dull red hot-spots on hijacker's ship slowly cool back to gunmetal grey. Her suit thermometer said it was at least minus 210 degrees outside but with almost no air out there, she knew cooling was not very efficient. After several minute the surface of the ship gradually started to look normal and possibly cool to the touch..

"Katherine, come on down. Not too close," Jason said as he started walking cautiously toward the damaged ship. "I'd like to see if there's any crew left and get them back to the Escalante's brig but I don't want this damn ship to explode just when we get there."

"Okay! Why would it explode now?" Kitty yelled as she carefully made her way down the ice shelf and set her feet her down on the icy surface near Jason and the trawler.

"Who knows , maybe when it was damaged we hit something crucial. If the hull fails it could all go up."

From talking to Lex she remembered what he said that if the structural integrity failed the ship with normal air pressure inside could literally explode into the vacuum around it and the atmosphere on Europa was close to a vacuum. She watched as Jason approached the ship's rear air-lock and placed his hand on a panel next to the lock. He stopped and she could see that he was looking at the ice panorama in front of them. It was dimly lit although they had the full view of the sun although at this distance it was incapable of heating things up much. What light there was reflected off the glasslike ice walls of the cliffs. She wondered whether he saw something. She called, "Jason!

What do you see, the hijackers? Are they coming back?" There was silence for a second.

"No, no hijackers, but this area is familiar. I think we Ice Rangers used to have maneuvers in this place. I'm sure of it," he said.

"I'm glad it's old home week, Jason, but we should get into this ship before it blows," she answered.

"Of course, I'm sorry." He motioned to Kitty to stay put. She could see him switch to ship communicator,

"Cody, you there?"

"Right on Jason," Williams answered. Kitty could hear it also.

"See if you can raise anyone in this tug and get the airlock pumped."

After a few seconds, they heard from Williams, "No can do, all I get is an open signal. They don't answer. Doesn't look good."

Jason moved to the side of the air-lock and Kitty could see him remove the cover adjacent to the lock.

"All right, I've got access to the manual control. At least I can get in. Gauges look normal, and pressure inside is still about atmospheric. The interlock seems to be functioning but I think we have to wait for the pressure to lower inside before we try it. The ship could break apart any minute."

"Jason, that's crazy!" Kitty said startled. "That means we wait to make sure they're all dead inside. It'll be like the vacuum we have out here. What if survivors don't have suits on, they wouldn't last ten seconds without one. We're going in now young man. Open the air-lock."

Kitty didn't mean to sound as bossy as she did but maybe Jason's remark a while back that she was an older woman got to her. He was the young man. Now she giving him orders. She was acting like the older woman he thought she was. It felt right. It was right. Besides how could they have risked so much just to let those inside suffocate or freeze, or worse.

"All right, Katherine, but what if this is a trick too and they're waiting for us with loaded stunners."

Kitty was shocked by this possibility and a little angry.

"If they do I'll melt the whole ship into one giant puddle."

"Good girl," he said as he twisted the first lock handle.

As soon as Jason had the first door of the air-lock opened Kitty breathed a sigh of relief. Stepping inside there was nothing but silence, with her hand she indicated Jason should follow. They gingerly stepped further into the lock interior as if they didn't want to disturb the ship and closed the outer door. Jason manually opened a valve and when the outside and inside pressure were the same the inside door opened. "Katherine, pressure inside is holding, it looks like we can get in but we better be quick before the whole thing blows."

The door slid open and revealed a cargo bay with a thick grey smoke hanging over stacks of boxes labeled, 'Au' and some 'Eb'. Jason turned a small knob on his belt control. It apparently opened a vent by his head bubble. He immediately shut it.

"It stinks of plastic, burning plastic. This is toxic. Let's get out of here, I see no one so far."

He's clearly worried about the ship breaking apart, Kitty thought. "If you're right we have seconds. If the ship explodes I don't think we'll remember. Let's do it."

"The bridge should be through that bulkhead." Jason proceeded to the far end of the compartment they were in. Kitty was right with him.

None of the electronic controls seemed to work so he and Kitty struggled with the door, finally opening it and before them one crew members lay sprawled on the bridge deck by a slowly spreading fire and The Captain lay face down by the control panel, blood running over the panel.

Kitty ran to the first one on the floor and looked at Jason, "Dead!"

"The Captain, too. Not much we do with them. When the stunner backfired it got them."

As he said that a loud creak resounded throughout the ship but then nothing more, silence. Kitty thought an ominous silence.

Jason paused for a second, listening to the creeks and groans of the ship. "I'm sorry Katherine," he said quickly, " but I was in an exploding ship once before. I never want to do that again."

Through their audio connection to the bridge they heard, Adams shouting, "Katherine, Jason, get your asses back here, we're starting to see pieces rip off that ship. It's ready to break apart. Get back here!"

As they were leaving the damaged ship, Cody Williams, with his exo-suit on rushed past them back into the trawler to the hijacker console.

"No better time than now to dump their files." He inserted a small chip and made several computer commands.

Kitty yelled after him "You're crazy Cody, get out of here!"

"It's the only chance we have of finding who they were." He pulled the chip from the computer and he and Kitty hurried back to the lock and the Escalante.

Kitty, finally inside the Escalante, looked around and realized Jason had not returned.

"No Jason?" she said and wildly looked around.

Adams spoke up, "No, we thought he was with you."

In spite of his fears that boy is going to get blown up again, Kitty thought. She told Sadoka to hold the lock open until she made sure Jason was back. The Escalante lock started to close as she sprinted back to the hijackers' wreck of a ship. There in spite of his fears was Jason , staring out of the ships viewports looking out onto the ice.

"Katherine, I'm sure. This is where I used to explore when I was a Ranger. I'm sure of it."

"That's nice Jason, but you're the one who doesn't want to get blown up again. Let's get out of ..." She didn't finish her thought as the entire roof of the ship split open with a thunderous crack lifting both of them off their feet and in the rush of air, sweeping them out onto the ice.

Chapter Twenty-One

"Katherine...Katherine! Wake up !*"* It was a familiar voice, *"Enough of this reverie. You are in danger of freezing to death if you don't adjust your suit."* It was her alter ego, her friend, Carg.

"But it's fun to dig your toes into this fine sand of the desert and feel the warm ..." Kitty thought back but began to stir as she noticed that the warm desert sand had vanished and she was lying on a bed of ice, and indeed her feet were cold, freezing cold. With a jerk she reached down to her temperature control and found it in the off position and after a few thoughts as to what she should do she finally set it to normal temp. Her crash landing must have thrown it into the off position. That was an easy way to die without even knowing it.

"Carg, thank you, I was dreaming I was back on earth."

"Katherine, you were knocked unconscious." Carg was genuinely concerned Kitty realized.

"Thank you Carg, I dreamt I was warm and back home and none of this had happened."

She remembered the loud sound and little else but knew what had happened when she looked back at the shell of the hijackers' trawler. One whole side of the ship had blown out. And Jason! Where was he? She quickly looked around. "Jason," she called. To her great relief she saw him another thirty meters away near the edge of a crevasse lodged against an ice out-cropping, half covered with snow, but he wasn't moving.

"Jason! Are you all right?" There was no answer. "Jason! Jason!" He stirred. "Jason!" she called again.

Over her comm link she heard, "Katherine, it's here! I was sure this was the right place." It was Jason.

From the Escalante the voice of Cody and then Captain Adams rang out into their Comm systems. "Are you all right? Jason! Katherine! We saw what happened! You two what's going on? Answer!"

Kitty realized the Comm control to the Escalante was on.

"I'm okay," she answered, "I don't know about Jason. Jason!" she called out again.

"We found it. The site. . . I think I broke my arm. Ahhh!" a cry of pain, "It must be broken but this is the site."

"Katherine what is he talking about? He sounds delirious." Kitty realized that was Captain Adams on the comm link.

"Captain, he thinks this is the site of some games he was playing as a Ranger."

"No, they weren't games. We were on a deployment to the 109 crevasse and this is it." Jason was explaining, but between his pain and excitement, he barely was understood. "This is where the accident happened. Captain this is the Crevasse. It makes sense the hijackers would be here, this place is just off the main trail between Ilandia and the mining colonies. Your Laura's got to be here . . . somewhere."

Once Kitty felt the suit temperature get back to normal she managed to stand and, amidst an aching back but no broken bones, find her way over to Jason who was now sitting up, his right arm cradled by his waist, dusting the snow off with his left .

"Katherine, Look there." He pointed down into the depths of the crevasse. "See that dark area."

Straining her eyes, she indeed did see some kind of dark speck at least fifty meters down into the canyon. Was it an illusion, just a weird refraction of the dim light. She couldn't tell.

"Jason, your arm."

"It's not bad. Ahhh...", the sound of excruciating pain, "as long as I don't move it." He looked around and then at Kitty.

"Katherine, I have to go down there . . . but I can't get down there and someone..."

Before he finished, she knew what he had in mind.

"No thank you. Not down into that hole. It has no bottom. Look down there, it's all ice and you can't see the bottom and it's cold! Are you crazy!"

He must be delirious if he wants her to take a closer look and that meant down into the depths, tens of meters down into the ice cavern. But she knew Lex or Adams couldn't do it, and the others had to stay with the Escalante and with a sinking feeling she realized that if ever they were to find the Captain's wife that left her. Before she could think of a good reason not to get down there Jason switched to the Escalante Comm system.

"Captain, follow us with the ship and get the winches ready, Katherine is going down into a crevasse to get a look. She's spotted something."

Adams answered, "Katherine, is that right? You're going down to take a look? Do you need the radar probe."

Jason answered, "No, Captain. Visual should be good. She will need a sling seat on the winch."

Here we go again, she thought, I've been volunteered. She wished she could say no but if it was the body of Laura, someone had to get down there but it would have been nice even to have had a say in going down into that frozen canyon. She could refuse, she knew, but she also knew she wouldn't. As long as she had some Terran strength left it might work.

Kitty carefully made her way along the edge of the ice shelf to get a closer look at the dark spot which now looked only about thirty meters down. Jason followed holding his injured arm with his good arm. In the distance they could see the Escalante powering its way towards them.

"Katherine," Carg appeared again dressed in her version of the thermal suit Kitty was wearing. She peered down into   the

crevasse. *"My, that looks dangerous. Katherine, you just make sure I don't lose my bet with my group leader. There's a lot riding on this."*

"Carg, you're coming down this hole with me. If I freeze down there that's the end of your project and I won't care a bit. You stay with me"

Kitty thought to herself that there certainly is a lot riding on this, her life for instance. She knew this is not what she wanted to do but there was no one else. All she had to do was ride the sling down, check it out and ride it back up. In a way she felt empowered.

"Captain!" Jason continued. "Can someone get out and bring us the fusion torches, maybe Lex? They're by the wrecked ship's air lock. We may need them here."

Kitty thought the word 'we' might mean that Jason could do something to help, but every time he made the slightest effort his face showed the pain he was in. It was all going to be Kitty. So be it, she thought, me and my alter ego or guardian angel or whatever she was.

Down into the bottomless ice pit to look at a smudge in the ice.

****

Brace Adams sat back in his Captains chair but admitted to himself that he didn't feel very much like a Captain now. He knew now he certainly would have failed in his search for Laura and probably would have died in the attempt. His neuropathy was progressing far faster than he expected. He wasn't sure he could even walk across the bridge deck now.

Jason and Katherine were heroes in his mind. But is what they've spotted Laura? It looked like her. He'd know for certain now in a matter of hours. After five years! Then what? That he didn't know. Could she be revived with no permanent damage or would there just be a funeral or worse some perpetual care institution?

At that moment they all felt the vibration of an approaching cruiser. Cody announced it was Europan Security. He had shifted to his Comm console and flipped on the outboard cameras and they could see the ship lumbering over the ice banks, a large trawler with obvious armaments mounted on their forward and aft turrets and insignias of the Europan command. It pulled alongside the remnants of the wrecked trawler which now was only an empty shell. In the process of disintegrating, several oxygen tanks must have gotten loose and they could see brilliant flashes of light where components were melting and fusing in the pure oxygen stream.

"They have identified themselves, Captain," Cody announced, "and their Commander wants to talk to us."

"Put him on," Adams said.

Cody flipped a switch and the image of the Commander holding his vidpad appeared above Cody's console.

"From what I read it's you Brace, Brace Adams, old friend."

"John Champion! We have to meet way out here?"

"I haven't seen you since Academy days. How the hell are you? I have the report from your Comm Officer, but what happened here?"

"John, we intercepted a garbled distress call from what we thought was a merchant ship," he pointed to the remnants of the burning hull. "My Comm engineer managed to decipher it and we detoured to the attack site. Much like we figured, there was a merchant ship but it was a trap. Fortunately a few of my people scared off the hijackers. It retreated in their shuttle and two of my crew are still out there so be careful."

"Brace, I know the kind of trawler you're in. It has no weapons, how did they do that?"

"It's a long story, but you're familiar with the fusion Ice cutter used around here. Well, my guys nearly cut the hijackers in half with those torches. Let's say those bastards left in a rush when half their stunners were cut in pieces and the other half were turned into mush. Then our people started to cut into the hijacker's hull. We couldn't send a distress call of our own until we stopped the attack. There were no survivors on board the trawler but some of the hijackers   did escape. We didn't pursue."

"Very impressive. Yes, you were lucky."

Champion had spotlights trained on Jason and Kitty in their thermal suits. "I see two out in their underwear. Amazing. Someday I want to hear more about that. Right now we're on the hijacker's trail and we'd like to get them before they enter the ice tunnels. Once they do that we'll lose them in that maze. Let's meet for brandy later on. Send us the last shuttle position and direction of retreat, any coordinates of their movement. Right now one of our satellites is tracking them.

"One more thing, Brace, you should unload the cargo from the wreck. If it's what I think it is there's quite a valuable shipment of metals stolen in the past week and if that's where it is, return it to Ilandia. I think there's some kind of reward for that. Congratulations... and Brace, I hope all is well with you."

Adams answered, "I'll give you the skinny over brandy." But Adams knew he would be lucky to even walk on his own to the Space lounge bar in Ilandia and wondered if he'd even be alive by then.

Chapter Twenty-Two

"Katherine, how in the world did you get the courage to do this?" Carg, still in her thermal suit, said this while holding on to the winch cable, one foot on Kitty's seat, the other foot waving in air trying to push Kitty's seat away from the ice wall but to no avail. In the cradle, Kitty was slowly lowering herself down into the crevasse. She had the winch control in one hand and was trying to keep herself from crashing into the ice wall with both feet and her other hand.

"You might as well concede," Kitty thought, *"You've lost the bet. We're both going to tumble down into the pit and die."*

"Don't joke! I don't like heights especially when all I can see is darkness down below. This is terrible. There's no bottom to this hole."

"I'm getting the hang of this, maybe we won't fall. In fact this seat is comfortable and I have good control of how fast I go down. And I don't have courage. I've decided you're right. I'm just dumb enough to think I can do this."

"No, Katherine. I've decided I'm *wrong. It's courage. You can't be that dumb."*

Kitty closed her eyes for just a second to let that remark pass and on opening them Carg was gone. She felt that now she might get on with checking out this dark smudge and be free of distracting insults for a while. She began to lower herself further into the depths.

"Katherine," Jason was standing above her on the edge of the crevasse, "be careful of the ice shelves. They could tip you over if you hit them."

"Thank you, I'll watch," she said but avoiding ice clumps jutting out from the walls was just one of her worries. She was barely able to see the hazards as she descended. There were head lights on her suit but they cast too many shadows and strange reflections.

"I'm now almost facing the ice wall and I see some kind of smudge way deep into the ice. The surface is too encrusted to see detail. I'll need some good lighting down here. Suit lights aren't enough." She was now hanging in her seat cradle nearly thirty meters from the surface above, face to face with a wall of ice that had streaks ground into its face very likely by tidal movements. It distorted the view of anything hidden inside.

"Maybe the fusion torch can smooth out the wall so you can see what's there. We've done that at times when I was an Ice Ranger to make windows for our ice houses. You just sweep the flame parallel to the face, enough to smooth it. Sometimes when you get it right it looks like glass."

"I wish you could be down here Jason. I'll try. Send some lights down."

"Will do. I wish I could help but, Ahh! . . . No I can't. I'll send down some flood lights. Just be careful with the torch, you don't want to cut the winch line and wind up at the bottom of the pit."

Kitty thought that last was good advice but all it did was make her more jittery.

Carg appeared again but by this time Kitty was so used to these sudden appearances of her alter ego that she didn't jump in surprise. She was dressed in a bulky bright purple ski jacket and wore sleek looking boots and gloves although Kitty guessed she didn't feel the cold, she was being theatrical.

"Carg, be useful and see if you can see more into the ice wall than I can. I just see a smudge. Could it be a person."

"I can't see anything more than you can. I do notice things

that you may have overlooked, but not this time. Are any of your friends going to help? Or are they just going to leave you down here, dangling above certain death?"

While that was unnecessary from Carg, the thought ran through her mind that if they had to speed back to Ilandia they might just leave her. No, Adams wouldn't do that, he's been thinking of this search for years and this is it. This is not the time to become paranoid. Relax.

"Katherine," it was Jason above. "I've got the torch and some lights . I'm lowering them on another winch. Careful, I've set the torch for a two meter flame. Is that enough?"

"It should be." she reached for the line as it approached her. "Got it."

Carg, still in her heavy jacket asked, *"What will you do now?"* Kitty positioned herself along the side of the wall. She set up the lights and hefted the fusion gun to her waist. *"I think I wipe the flame up and down the face of the wall."* Saying this she reset the flame for three meter range and pulled the trigger. The neat blue flame shot out and wherever it touched the ice it cut a swath. She waved the flame up and down the ice face and gradually moved it closer and closer to the surface. She could see layer after layer of ice melt away and freeze some few meters down into the canyon. The face she was working on slowly became smooth and she could see reflections of the opposite cavern wall.

Carg was hanging on to Kitty's seat and was stretching to get a view through the now shiny wall of ice. Her alter ego craned her neck to try to see into the wall and as Kitty swung her seat more towards the front; Carg's mouth dropped open, eyes wide.

"Come look!" she said.

Kitty managed to position her seat around and with her feet guided herself to the front of her newly polished ice wall. There about a meter into the wall was a body, totally encased in solid ice like a fly caught in an ice cube. It was a woman still in her grey thermal suit lying on her side, she had tried to stay warm by huddling up into a fetal position. Half expecting the figure to reach out to her, she was frozen solid but looking straight at Kitty, her eyes still partially open, skin bluish white in color. This had to be Laura! Could she ever be brought back to life? What was Adams thinking? How could they even get her out of there? Was this to be a funeral?

Looking over Kitty's shoulder Carg appeared, *"You've found her. I would never have believed it possible with such primitive methods. Impressive! Now what?"*

"Good question, the Captain has to decide on the next move," Kitty thought.

Through her comm link she heard Jason first,

"Katherine, what is it?" She didn't answer at first thinking this was some other mental communication, but no, this was coming from Jason still standing on the edge of the crevasse above her.

"Katherine, have you found something?" This time it was Captain Adams. "Switch on your camera."

She had forgotten the camera attached to her head visor. She switched it on and heard the Captain draw in his breath and he whispered,

"Oh my God! Laura. It's Laura!"

Chapter Twenty-Three

Frozen for five years, encased in ice that measured 200 below zero, Laura could last in place another few hours everyone thought, but not another year. Every year meant a loss of nearly ten percent in her survivability index or so Cody Williams had found from sorting through the documented cases of frozen humans in Ilandia's unforgiving cold ... and there were sixty eight over the years. To leave her as she was, meant giving up hope of resuscitation, in other words, a permanent ice burial.

Instead of joy for having found his wife's body, Brace Adams sank into his chair,

"Now what? Now what?" he muttered, more to himself than to the others.

"Do you hear that?" Carg said as she appeared standing next to Kitty who had managed with relative ease to get back to the bridge of the Escalante. *"He's got to get her out of there. That's all there is to it,"*

"It's not that simple," Kitty thought. *"She could have all sorts of problems when we thaw her out. Even if she could be brought back to life, she might not even recognize him. You know, mental problems."* Carg was a bit thoughtless about the situation.

"Katherine, I'm sorry. I forgot you people don't have the medical skill we have. On our world she would be totally herself when we thawed her out. We have cold zones in our world and some of our explorers have been frozen like your Laura for a hundred of your years. We have ways of bringing them back even after that. One thing for certain, you've got to cut her free of that ice burial if you want her back."

Carg was the silent for a few seconds and then said, *"Let me work on something I've been thinking about."* Saying this, Carg vanished.

Much as she knew no one could see her alter ego, Kitty still looked around to see if anyone noticed. There was no reaction from the others. She then tried what she considered a strong thought.

"Carg, what the hell are you planning?"

The Captain, barely able to walk, struggled over to a side cabinet and broke out a bottle of '26 Venusian brandy. It seemed to be his favorite drink.

"To you, Katherine". He offered all of his so called crew glasses and toasted her. "I knew I did the right thing getting you on board the Escadril but I didn't know you would be such a brave soul challenging the ice the way you did. Who else could have crawled down into that cavern? Not me, certainly."

He looked to Jason, "And without you, Jason, this never would have happened." He sipped his drink and continued, "to you others, Lex, Sadoka and Cody. You are the best. You've managed the travel across this damned planet...all right, moon... and got us to the right place in one piece. He put down his drink and settled back in his chair, sinking even lower than he was before.

"But after five years, what do I do now?"

The others looked at each other not knowing what to say. Finally Kitty spoke up, "Captain, it makes no sense to just leave her there." Kitty motioned with her head to the ice crevasse, "and there's good chance she can be brought back to life. In the worst case," she knew the Captain was in no condition to take care of a disabled Laura,

"I will take care of her if she needs help. That's a pledge. Captain, I've said this before, but you risked your career and maybe more bringing me on board. Without that escape from Luna I'd be a mental disaster case or in the Venus stockade. I owe you."

The Captain managed a smile and said, "But what can you do?"

Using his left hand, Lex waved in the direction of   the Crevasse, "It can be done, Captain. I've seen bigger blocks cut from the side of ice mountains outside Ilandia. The fusion torches can do it and Katherine knows how to use them. We can talk her through it and we'll have your wife's body in our cargo bay by tomorrow."

"Alone?" Adams asked. " You and Jason are both disabled."

"Captain," Cody interrupted, " There's nothing more I can do here." He got up from his chair, "and I'm tired of sitting at this console. I can help out there. We've given a full report to Europan security and they're on the trail of the hijackers . If they try to contact us I can patch in any incoming to our Comm lines. You have to have two of us out there."

Adams nodded. "All right! If it can be done let's try." He seemed to a have a bit of that sparkle Kitty saw in him in the past. Maybe this would work out.

She re-attached her head bubble as Cody put on his thermal suit and bubble. Looking over her friends she realized Cody was the only able bodied man left of the crew. There was Sadoka but she was really too old to go traipsing over ice dams and boulders. Lex and Jason were dealing with injured arms and the Captain was barely able to walk, If Laura was to be cut from the ice, she had to do it. As she and Cody proceeded to the air lock she realized she was feeling a need to free this trapped woman. Seeing her frozen in place, her eyes open, staring at her, brought up a feeling of empathy to this trapped figure. Maybe she was unconsciously trying to free herself from her own troubles. Perhaps Carg, who had access to her unconscious, could analyze that better than she could. Where was Carg anyway? When you need your alter ego she doesn't show up.

Sadoka maneuvered the Escalante closer to the edge of the Crevasse and released all four winches she had control over. Once onto the ice Kitty and Cody brought the cables to the edge of the ice canyon and with the fusion torch on her back, Kitty slowly lowered herself down to the wall she had polished. Seeing Laura as before should not have startled her, but she looked so lifelike Kitty felt like yelling to her to relax, that they would have her out of there in a few hours.

Lex and Jason had worked out the cutting plan. She ignited her torch and first cut vertical swaths on each side of the block of ice that would contain Laura's body. Then she cut another vertical but at an angle to the first and as planned, when she approached the bottom of the first cut, the slab of ice broke off and fell. With almost no air she heard nothing as the block careened off the sides of the ice canyon down into unknown depths. Then she carved off the other side. More carefully she carved grooves into each side of the wall and Cody swinging off his winch seat managed to lash the third and fourth cables around what would be the block containing Laura. Then she did the same with the horizontal. Bottom first and then top. She now had an ice shelf cantilevered out of the wall. Avoiding the metal cables she slowly cut into the top of the block. As the torch line cut deeper into the ice she realized that if the block broke in half, so would Laura's body be cracked in half. She shut the torch.

Cody, hanging from his winch seat and an outcropping of ice, looked at her,

"What's wrong. It looks good so far."

"Cody, if the block breaks off the wall the wrong way we could lose her."

As she said this the ice block cracked off the wall and was caught be the two cables on either side but it held together. They had it! A block of ice one by one meter on its side and two meters across. Laura was intact folded inside this giant ice cube.

Chapter Twenty-Four

Sadoka seemed to have a feather touch as she maneuvered the Escalante to within a meter of the edge of the ice cliff and then extended its hoist arms. The winch cables ran over these arms in pulleys and on signals from Kitty they slowly lifted the block away from the wall. The ice canyon could be a mile deep and if the block dropped that would be the end of their rescue effort but the cables held and they lifted this giant ice cube containing Laura out of the depths, over the ice surface, and suspended it high above their heads, swinging gently. Kitty and Cody managed to steady it and guide it back to the cargo compartment all the while wondering if it could break loose and fall on either one of them or both, a fitting end to this misadventure . But the hoists worked as planned and the block slowly made its way into the trawler.

"You can't raise the temp in here," Kitty said as Cody closed the Cargo doors and turned on the air. "We should try to keep it as cold as possible. If it gets too warm a crack might start and spread."

"You're right, hadn't thought about that. It should be ice eleven and at some temp it makes a phase change to ice ten. I hope not soon," Cody said, and then looked at Kitty. " I can't believe how you used that torch. You were like an artist with it."

"One of my many talents . Thanks. Once I got the hang of that thing it was easy. Burning up the hijacker's ship helped, those bastards." Her anger returned for just a few seconds.

"That's the language I like to hear. Tell it like it is." Carg appeared sitting on the block of ice. She was wearing one of Kitty's favorite summer outfits. Something she dug up in Kitty's mind from far more pleasant times. It was disconcerting at first because she was sitting on that block of ice with bare legs and it was more than two hundred degree below zero. *"You did a fantastic job in cutting that body out of the ice. I showed the visuals to my people and they raved about it. They are supporting me now. You really caught their interest."*

Visuals? Kitty became immediately suspicious and wondered what this figment had in mind. More insults or some kind of scheme to get her research published? She found that it was possible to isolate some thoughts from Carg but it took an effort. Casual thoughts she could pick up on, but that reinforced an old lesson -- think before you speak, but in this case, think before you think.

"Carg, I don't know what you have in mind but I'm not open to any more thoughts of joining Madam Canzioni in her business. If I ever have a love life again it'll be mine, not yours."

"All right, I can make up a good part of that. Sadly, I can imagine what yours has been like." Carg answered surprising Kitty. *"But I do like the way you're taking charge. You've given me a good start on my work already."* Her alter ego slipped off the block and bent over staring at the body of Laura. Kitty knew she shouldn't feel embarrassed but Carg was using her body and her bottom was aiming right at Cody. After all he couldn't see her! But Cody was staring at exactly where Carg was bending over. Was this something perhaps he could imagine?

Kitty decided to pursue this. "Cody, what were you seeing?" she asked hoping to catch him off guard.

"Uh...nothing, just looking at our block of ice," he said and he turned towards the hoist and began loosening the cables. Kitty thought she saw a slight blush come over him but she couldn't be sure.

140

She looked back to Carg and she had changed into the thermal body suit, much as Kitty had on. It had to be that her alter ego had sensed how uncomfortable she was thinking that Cody was imagining her with barely anything on and in awkward positions.

"You've done it!" Carg said, *"I don't think my people could have done it better and I think she possibly can come back after five of your years if she has the right rescue treatments. You are a resilient species from what we know."*

What does she know? She's not telling, and what are the right rescue treatments. And how does she know about humans? Kitty thought in her protected way of thinking.

"Look Carg, isn't it about time you tell me what you know about us humans...and how did you find all this out. You can't have got it all from me."

"Katherine, Katherine." She hopped up on the block of ice and dangled her feet down. *"You deserve some answers. You remember I said we had visited your world many hundreds of years ago. That was when we first started using what you people call worm holes. We call them spatial jumps. After we learned that your world had sentient beings--present company excepted, we..."*

"Carg, that's it. I'm helping you get your research done and all you've done is insult me. No more!"

"You are right, no more, but we have a sharp sense of humor on my world. I won't do that anymore and besides you really are admirable in many ways. But don't forget you're not free and clear yet." Saying this she vanished and Kitty realized she never did tell anything more about humans.

Finally, Kitty thought, maybe a little respect from this alter ego. Not so much she realized from any great intelligence she's shown, that she admitted, but from her determination to survive. She understood now that she was a survivor. Here she was escaping prison, a dreadful operation and an assassination attempt, and now, almost certain death down a bottomless crevasse. What do you call

141

that? She was right though, someone still had a price on her head. But once she was back in civilization she could get that damned transponder out of her neck and then she'd really be free. Her part of the reward money would do nicely.

But how about Laura. She couldn't take her eyes off the sleeping figure, sleeping or frozen or dead. She didn't know which. What about Laura's chances. The Captain was right, though. Now what?

She turned to Cody, "We have to get the Captain. He should know we got her and she's here." She went back to staring at the immobile form in the ice.

"I agree. He needs that. I'll get a camera arranged," Cody said. "but she has to stay frozen until the Medics can get to her, that's the best we can do. Can't let her thaw. She's got to stay at near two hundred below zero."

Kitty thought for a second. Now was that Fahrenheit or Celsius? One always sounded worse than the other. Whatever, it was cold and she had to stay that way.

And where did Carg disappear to?

Chapter Twenty-Five

What a relief it was to get out of that thermal suit and wear something comfortable in an atmosphere that you could breathe and not worry about freezing to death. Kitty took a deep breath and slumped back into one of the only chairs available, the Captain's chair. He was not using it. She looked over to Lex and wondered if he too thought of that time in her room back on the Escadril when he helped her out of her suit. Now, look at him. He lost his arm trying to get her out of the way. Would he ever be interested in her again. Maybe later, she thought. They do make amazing mechanical arms, useful, but not like a real arm.

Adams was sitting in front of the view screen which had the image of Laura's frozen body. He seemed to be deep in thought. Kitty thought to herself that she too would be thinking about what to do now. The search was over. He had not planned for this moment and now he was faced with a decision.

"Captain," Cody called, "Katherine, everyone, come listen to this. It's a message that came in while we were out on the ice. It concerns you, Katherine." He flipped a switch and the view screen lit up with an image of John Champion, Captain of the Europan Security trawler which had found them hours back. He looked a bit more serious than he did before.

"Brace, I'm not sure this message can get through. We're on the other side of the escarpment 112 . Thanks to your people we have the hijackers. You did a good job of disarming them. With no weapons to fight back they didn't put up a fight, just gave up. But my Comm officer has found something strange. He's detected a signal, apparently it was riding on the carrier wave of our communication the last time we spoke. Of all things it's coming from a microbug that's on your ship. We've checked it out with Ilandia security and it's one they planted back when you were stopped by McNeil and Security on the Escadril. It was responding to a transponder carried by a Katherine DeLumiere."

At that everyone looked over to Kitty who had raised herself from her lethargy and was now wide awake at the mention of her name.

The message continued, "She's an escaped prisoner and a wanted revolutionary. They consider her dangerous. We have to meet and I'm forced to search your ship to find her. I don't appreciate that kind of work, but it's recorded and I have to check it out. Hold your position and I will call again when we get on the other side of the escarpment." The message ended.

They all looked at Kitty who now very much felt like a trapped animal. Lex spoke first, "I don't think we can hide anywhere this time. This ship doesn't have the shielding the Escadril had. They could find Katherine anywhere on this tub or within a kilometer around us."

Kitty thought for a moment that maybe they could leave her somewhere far from the ship but that was really scary. Alone on a frozen wasteland. She imagined being eaten by a polar bear but her rational side knew there were no animals on this world...or were there?

In response to a flashing diode, Cody turned to the Captain, "that's probably them now hailing us." He checked a few settings, "Yes, it's on their security channel."

Adams looked to Cody and he waved his hand. "Don't. Don't answer it." Then he turned to Sadoka, "Sadoka, full speed to Ilandia. If we can get there before he catches us, Katherine can make a run for it." He apparently had made a decision. "I'm not going to waste time stopping for Champion to search this ship. We know what he'll find." He nodded to Kitty. "But Laura, can't wait. Five years is enough."

"Captain," Jason woke up from the relaxant Sadoka had given him while she set his arm, "From what I remember, ice caught in a tidal upsurge sometimes is under tremendous pressure. When that's released, like when a block is cut out, stress fracture can start."

"All the more reason to not stop," Adams said.

"Aye, Aye sir" Sadoka said as she entered several commands into her engineering board system and they felt the acceleration of the trawler speeding up. "Course laid in for Ilandia. But Captain you know that Champion's ship is pretty fast. He may still find us before we get there."

"Yes," Adams said, "but it gives us some time to do some thinking. There may be something we can do. Katherine is no threat."

Kitty thought that yes she was no threat to anyone. But thinking back to Laura's ice block. The small fracture she saw starting might not be because of the temperature change, it could have been what Jason is talking about. If that's true there's no hope of a rescue. She glanced over to the thermometer gauge in the Cargo bay. It read two hundred and thirty below. The temp isn't changing. It's the pressure change! Jason is right!

She looked carefully at the view screen and indeed there were two other cracks starting. It was happening. Stress fractures!

"Katherine, I've been listening and it seems like you are in serious trouble now. That Captain Champion will probably stop this trawler and haul you away to some forsaken prison or ruin what's left of your brain. And those fractures are going to destroy this Laura." Carg had appeared and was listening in on their conversation but this time Kitty felt no loss of privacy nor any insult. What difference did it make if Carg knew the situation she and Laura were in. It was hopeless.

"Thank you, but this time I take no offence at your lack of delicacy. You are absolutely right. Insult me all you want."

"Please, you still don't understand our sense of humor. I mean no insult. You're supposed to insult me right back. I thought you knew that."

"Well, next time, but this may be the last time I'm able to talk to you before they drug me all out of reality and poor Laura will be ripped apart by the ice."

"You mean you weren't already drugged out...Oh excuse me. I'm doing it again. No more insults. But I have an option. Can you get back to the Cargo bay?"

Adams turned from his vigil by the image of Laura and looked at Kitty.

"Katherine, if you don't mind I'd like to sit in my chair."

Kitty immediately jumped up and moved to the side. The tone of his voice seemed to indicate that he was not giving up either. In spite of his disease he still seemed optimistic. Perhaps the possibility of Laura coming back to life was making a difference. He limped over to his chair.

"Sadoka, can we squeeze any more speed out of this tub?" he said.

"Sir, I can get a few more horsepower if we shut down life support in all rooms except the bridge area.

"Do it," he said. They all felt the increase in the sway and jolting of the Escalante as the speed increased.

"That helps, Captain. We've got seventy knots now, not bad, but I think the Security ship can do ninety. They'd catch us about twenty kilometers outside of Ilandia."

"The Captain, rubbed his chin in his hands, "We can hope that they hit a tidal fault," he said, only half-jokingly. Captain John Champion was his friend.

Cody had been playing with his console feeding the info cube he had removed from the hijackers in and other encryption tools and finally looked at Captain Adams,

"Sir! I have some of what the hijackers had on their computer , only the last few minutes' worth. It has some glitches but I can play it."

"Go ahead," Adams said.

" ... Mayday ... May ... That should set ... trap. All right ...Or...land, take to cover."

"Did you hear that?" Kitty said for everyone to hear.

"What? Didn't hear much of anything." Adams said.

"He said 'Orlando!' " Kitty snapped.

"Katherine, you're imagining. He said ' land'. Could have been anything." Lex said.

Somewhat consoled by Lex, Kitty still seemed frustrated. "I'm sure that's what he said...land ... he's talking to Orlando. The first part was the fake message and then he was talking to ..."

"Katherine," Lex took Kitty's arm. "You're imagining. He didn't say anything about an Orlando. Please relax. What you did out there was enough to stress anyone. Relax."

Carg looked at Kitty, *"Katherine forget about what he said, forget about that rat. Lex is right.*

I've got a solution to your troubles. You have to get back to the Cargo bay and your block of ice. That Laura will die if the cracks spread across her. I talked to my bosses and they've given me some time."

"Time? What are you talking about. Time? Time for what?"

"Katherine, I'm talking about time to use what you people call 'worm hole' technology. So get dressed and get to the Cargo Bay. Laura's waiting."

Chapter Twenty-Six

According to Carg, worm holes, as Terran science calls them, are spatial rifts that Carg's people have been using for hundreds of years already. It involves creating a tremendous amount of negative energy and injecting it into space somehow. Carg didn't know how that was done but if it's coordinated with directions in space the two regions can communicate and people can travel great distances in no time at all. That's how visitors from Carg's world visited earth and how they actually carried several Terrans back through the rift to Carg's world. She said there are some Terrans who live there still. They have their own colony and call it Mayland.

"Yes, Mayland!" Carg said, *"Most of the Terrans there are related to the original earthlings who were carried back. My people realized many years later that this was wrong and offered to return those people back to earth but most refused and wanted to stay on their Mayland. They preferred our world. A few went back but not many."*

"What's that got to do with Laura and me?" Kitty asked as she stepped out of the air lock into the Cargo bay. *"I hate this thermal suit."*

In her mind Kitty saw Carg move over to the block of ice and run her finger over the crack that was starting. She turned back to Kitty.

"They tell me, the specialists in this sort of thing, that if you let this crack keep going it will cut your Laura in half. That'll be the end of her."

"I know that! But what can we do?" Kitty said wondering what else Carg had in mind.

"We can open a worm hole right here and get the ice block through. We've got medical staff ready to free her. They're sure she can come back to life."

Kitty looked over to the ice block where Carg was standing and heard a loud crack as the fissure spread another few centimeters towards Laura's frozen body. Carg looked at it and then over to Kitty.

"Well?" she said.

Without a thought of the consequences Kitty simply reacted and said, *"Open a worm hole? What does that mean?"* They heard another crack of the ice, *"Do it! Do it!"*

The Cargo Bay is normally lit with a few diode lights giving it a dim glow but at that instant Kitty saw, at one end of the ice block, a small circle of light, no more than a few centimeters wide, begin to spread and turn into something like a tunnel entrance almost two meters across. Through the circle of light she could see some kind of activity, figures moving about, large instruments moving into the bright view. The circle approached the ice block and slowly moved to enclose one end of it. Carg called to Kitty from the far end of the ice block.

"Push! Let's get it into the opening."

Kitty leaned on the block and pushed as it slid totally into the circle of light and as she did she realized she also was standing in the worm hole, if that was what it was. She looked back and saw the dim interior of the Cargo Bay slowly get darker until it vanished and she was completely in a brightly lit room. Turning towards the front where all the activity was, she saw a figure standing before her. She was human at least humanoid with bright red hair flowing around her. She had woman's features, yet she was slightly taller than most women, dark, long red hair, large dark eyes, what Kitty imagined a fairy might look like, a rather impressive fairy. She had a black leather or plastic skin tight outfit on with heavy metal bands on each arm and she seemed to move gracefully as she pointed to the crew working on Laura. That had to be her.

"Am I dreaming or are you...Carg?"

"Welcome to my world, yes I'm Carg. I'm in my own body, although it was nice to use yours for my time in your world. It was a bit harder to move around, you are heavier, but this is me."

It had to be Carg. The insults never quit. If anything Kitty knew she had lost weight in the recent months and she wasn't as tall as this person. She finally was meeting the real Carg, insults and all.

Carg acknowledged the flurry of activity around the ice block that had Laura. There were several figures rushing about and using some kind of device that seemed to be sawing off the ice in small bits. They worked quickly through the large areas with ice chips flowing into moveable vents. The process slowed when they came close to Laura. In a matter of seconds they had most of the ice removed to within a few millimeters of Laura's body. It was fascinating to watch. There she was, a glistening body, still in her exo-suit, lying on her side. A mechanical arm swiveled into place and the remaining ice covering melted and two of the workers immediately attached what seemed like a series of electrodes to Laura, perhaps a dozen. These workers spoke to each other in some kind of guttural language that Kitty didn't understand.

"And this crew," Carg indicated those working on Laura, "are specialists in this kind of resuscitation." Carg was actually speaking.

"But Carg," Kitty seemed overwhelmed, "What am I doing here? What's happening?"

"This is my world, the perfect hiding place for you while your trawler is being searched. That Captain Champion arrived at your Escalante trawler just after you came down to the cargo bay."

"They're looking for me now? Are you going to keep us here? Me and Laura?"

Carg laughed, "Katherine, we learned years back not to do that anymore. You can stay if you want to. There's plenty of room for you in Mayland, and other humans there. I can show you. And you and Laura can go back to your world if you want. We may have to make some memory corrections, but it's possible. But you could start life anew here."

What was happening was frightening ... a whole new world, through the worm hole ... and for an instant Kitty was tempted. But it was all too strange. If this was real it would be so easy to forget her past life and start fresh and let everything else on her world play out without her. Then she thought of Captain Adams and the others. Adams was dying and Lex could only look forward to a mechanical arm for the rest of his life. Yet here, Laura might come back to life.

"I don't know what to do. You're the brainy one. At least that's what you told me. What should I do?" Kitty said.

****

On the Escalante Brace Adams confronted his old friend, John Champion. Champion had his search team scour the Escalante for the microbug that sent the signal that Kitty's transponder had been located. They found the bug and he handed it to Adams. It was a device no bigger than a match head.

"Brace, here it is. It was attached to one of your formal outfits in your cabin."

"Well how did it get there? You mean that bastard, McNeil, bugged me without me knowing." Adams was irritated.

"Well, you know these security types. Don't trust anyone. But we've searched and there's no transponder. We're sure of that. I think the damned thing misfired. It's certainly quiet now."

"That's no surprise," Adams said. "You're certain? I don't feel like being stopped again. I'd like to get these gold bars delivered. Next they'll accuse me of stealing them."

Champion smiled, "No, not after my report. But Brace I didn't know you were having problems," he pointed to Adam's legs.

Adams lifted his hand up to shake hands with Champion and it was visibly shaking.

"That damn accident started this whole nerve thing, some kind of neuromyeolitis. I can handle it, though."

"Well with the reward money that should get you the best medical care around. Maybe back on Earth."

"That's the hope. Thanks John." Adams knew that was just a facade. There was no cure for what he had. He knew that.

"But Brace, what I don't understand is that our DNA detector registered the presence of this Katherine DeLumiere."

Adams had enough presence of mind to simply reply, "Well John, this is a leased ship. I have no idea what happened before we got it." He knew he was being deceptive but he was convinced this hunt for DeLumiere was politically motivated and to his mind unfounded and unneeded.

Champion may have felt the same since he accepted the theory of the rented ship. It was logical and plausible.

Adams didn't mention their hunt for Laura. That would have opened up more questions about this search. And where had Katherine disappeared to. She had to be on the ship but Champion couldn't find her. That woman is a mystery.

An hour later, after Champion and the Security trawler had left, Lex opened the view screen onto the Cargo bay and stepped back in surprise.

"Where 's the ice block? It's gone!" he turned to the others, "It's gone!"

"What happened?" He shouted as if someone knew what was going on.

The others, Jason, Cody and Sadoka looked up and ran to the screen. Adams hobbled there as best he could.

"It's gone!" Adams whispered, more to himself. "But look the gold bars are still there. All the metal... and Katherine's gone...what's going on? Champion checked every millimeter of this tug. I know him, but what would he do with a block of ice. He couln't take with him."

"Can't be him, Sadoka added. I had no reports of the Cargo Door opening. Only that he and some technician went down there and came back in a few minutes. I saw them a on the vid screen."

Cradling his broken arm, Jason said, "Help me into a suit. I have to see what happened. Maybe there's something."

"Help me too, Damn it," Adams said as he managed to get to the suit hangers. Lex and Cody helped him with the suit and got themselves ready. How could a ton block of ice disappear?

"Captain," Sadoka, still operating the ship controls, called to those already in the cargo bay, Captain Adams, Lex and Jason. "I've checked the exterior air-lock doors and the circuits are working. They haven't been opened since the ice block was brought in but we have video of Katherine moving the block to your left and then nothing more. They disappear from view. I don't understand."

Jason bent close to the floor while Lex tried as best he could to support the Captain.

"The ice tracks stop right here," Jason said and he pointed to ice skid marks that ended abruptly. No evidence of anything. The trail just ends." They looked to the left and all they could see were boxes of erbium and gold metal. "Where did she move that block? How could she do that, is she that strong and where could she put it anyway?"

Chapter Twenty-Seven

Kitty watched as the technicians hovered over Laura's body with its many newly attached electrodes. From where she was standing she could feel the warm glow of the light they were bathing her in. Probably infrared, she thought, but more than that. It had something purple in the light and it seemed to flicker. But Laura's been frozen for five years, certainly they're doing more than simply warming her up.

With hair that swirled around her body and with her dark eyes glowing Carg looked over to Laura's body. She pointed to several technicians.

"Once they switch on the modulation circuits your Laura should react. Although I think at first any movement will be just reflexes kicking in. Then she'll probably start shivering. It takes a while to regain consciousness and to get back to normal and even longer to get all memory back. Maybe several of your weeks."

Carg turned to Kitty, "Have you decided if you'll stay here, you'd like Mayland and maybe even find a decent Mate there. I know you. You'll get in trouble in your world."

"What makes you think I won't get into trouble on your world? What is this Mayland, anyway?"

"I told you. We used to visit earth a long time ago. It goes back hundreds of years when our first explorers were visiting different planets using these spatial rifts ... worm holes. They took people from your world and brought them back here."

"That's called kidnapping!"

154

"Strictly speaking, you're right, but the humans here in Mayland seem to have a life that many of my own people envy. We transplanted lots of the animal life from your terran world so they could survive and they've done very well. They seem to enjoy life here and only rarely does one of them want to go back to your Earth. We do take them back."

Still entranced by the activity about Laura, Kitty looked in surprise at Carg.

"Carg, I can't stay here. This is your world, mine is back there. And I have no interest in finding a man right now."

"Not even with Lex? From what our medics have told me we can get him his real arm in a month or so."

Kitty paused a few seconds to think about that. His own arm! That would be so much better than something mechanical besides she was the cause of him losing it. She did have a warm glow thinking of Lex and their times together.

Carg continued, "The Assembly has given me few more minutes of worm hole time and he could be here with you."

"You'd kidnap him?"

"Of course not, ...Oh!... just a minute." Some kind of squawk came out of a small device Carg had on her collar. Something in her own language. There was silence followed by what could only be described as a tirade from whomever she was talking to. Carg winced when it finally let up. And then she argued back in just as strong a voice followed by more shouting and arguing from the other side. She finally calmed down, "Moving Laura's block of ice cost too much and they're furious. The verdict is I've spent too much money already but ... after a little persuasion, I got them to open the hole long enough to get you through to your world and then let you convince Lex to come back with you."

Kitty knew this could be a life changing event. She and Lex might make it but on a world billions of kilometers away from Earth. That wouldn't be so bad except her life was here, as wretched as it was. Didn't one of the ancients say that the purpose of life is the struggle. Maybe they were right. Struggle she has. But then again, wouldn't it be nice to think about other things than just trying to stay alive, trying to avoid the police, and that's what she's been doing for the last year. Damn that Orlando the rat. He's the cause of all her troubles and if he was the hijacker and that Captain Champion caught him, wouldn't it be nice to see him finally go to prison or get zapped as Ella would have done. Ella. Where is she now? And Madam Canzioni. And Captain Adams fighting his own body. He probably doesn't have that long to go.

The argument and counter-arguments continued going through Kitty's mind. Maybe Carg was right and she had been a bit too naive or dumb and that's why she has all these problems. But still life a billion kilometers from earth! Would she be any smarter there? And Maybe Lex has other ideas. It all had to be a dream. A bad dream. But then, maybe a good dream.

Breaking the silence, more squawking came through Carg's collar piece.

"Katherine, we can't wait any longer, we have to use our negenergy soon or we'll lose it. I have to get the worm hole open now if you want to get Lex here, and you should get back to the Escalante. If Lex doesn't want to go through you can still come back. You have to decide."

This seemed like an impossible thing to decide. On Europa, and being rich with the reward money, things might be different. She had to go back there . Some surgeon could certainly be bribed to take that transponder out of her neck and surely Madam Canzioni could arrange that. And then there was what family she had back in Eritrea. They probably already had given her up as dead. She knew what she had to do.

"Open sesame, Carg!"

"What's that mean?" Carg was stymied.

"It's an ancient saying, it means open the worm hole."

156

****

"There's no way Katherine could get that ice block out of here. The tracks stop right here," Jason said as he pointed to skid marks that ended abruptly. No evidence of anything else." As they stared at the stacked boxes, a bright circle of light began to form. At first a few centimeters across but it grew to two meters of blinding light and through it walked Kitty.

"Captain, Lex, Jason. Just the people I want to see."

Chapter Twenty-Eight

Seeing the Captain leaning on Lex, and her friends, Cody and Jason kneeling there in the Cargo bay, all saying nothing intelligible with mouths open, staring at her, Kitty, walking calmly out of the worm hole, realized she must look like some apparition, in some ways she felt like a ghost who had come back from the underworld. No it was an advanced world, strange because of that, but according to Carg, her world, a real world. Just a thousand years ahead of the Terran world.

She looked back through the worm hole into the hospital room of Carg's world and Laura was already there sitting up on the table shivering. They had her back! Alive!

"There!" she said, "Laura's alive! Can you see that?" She pointed back into the glowing circle. "They did it. She's alive."

Still cradling his broken arm, Jason strained to look into the bright circle of light. "I see something, people I think someone's there, several ... is that Laura on the table? What is this?"

"This is all an illusion." Lex said, still propping up the Captain. "I don't understand. Some kind of holographic projection? Katherine, what's going on? You disappeared. Now here you are like some holy spirit appearing in a halo of divine light. Where did you go?"

Cody stepped closer to the circle, "There are people in there!" He pointed to Laura on the exam table, "Is that Laura, free of the ice?"

The Captain straightened, "Laura! What?" He said and seemed to be regaining strength by using her name.

158

"Look, it's all very strange," Kitty said trying to explain, even to herself. "It's not a hologram. It's real. It's another world through that tunnel, a real world. You all know I've been accused of delusions and having some kind of spiritual advisor. Well she's real, her name is Carg and she's from that world. She and I, we slid Laura's ice block through this tunnel... she says it's a worm hole into her planet."

Cody took notice, "I've heard of worm holes, but I thought they were stuff of far out theorists with wild imaginations. Is that what this is? I don't believe it."

Kitty walked over to the Captain and took his hand. "It's real. They call it a spatial rift. It connects our two worlds; the two regions of space can be billions of kilometers apart." She looked him in the eyes, "And see, that is Laura. They've got Laura back." She pointed back into the circle of light, " There she is . She's recovering. They're thousands of years ahead of us. Captain, Laura's going to be okay." A slight smile crossed his face.

"Laura! Okay? She's alive ?" he whispered and Kitty realized the Captain was barely himself. That disease was acting more quickly than anyone expected.

From speakers above their heads the voice of Sadoka broke through.

"All of a sudden I see Katherine appear." She was intent on the strange happenings in the Cargo bay. "How did that happen? What's going on."

"First the ice block disappears, then Katherine is gone and now Katherine is back. What's happening."

"Sadoka!" Kitty shouted back. "We don't exactly know ourselves. I can't explain it but I've been through a worm hole? Does that make sense?" Sadoka backed away from the view port, a surprised look on her face.

"You people must be playing games down there." Now her expression seemed to be one of anger. "Give me the skinny on what's happening!"

159

Lex shouted back, "We don't know!"

Sadoka, the engineer, the practical engineer, shouted back, "I don't know what all you people have been smoking and I don't want to be crass, but who gets the reward money if you all disappear like Katherine did. I'm coming down there. "

Still fascinated by the circle of light, Cody moved closer to its rim and stuck his arm into the tunnel and cautiously waved his hand inside,

"It doesn't feel like another world," he said. "What?" And withdrew his arm in surprise as Carg had clasped his hand and walked out with him, into the Cargo bay, her hand still in his. He stared at her apparently in awe as she approached him. In the background the circle of light outlined her fairy-like form.

Carg slowly walked towards Lex and the Captain.

"I feel like I know you all, but only through Katherine's eyes," she said. "But what she said is true. I am from another world several billion kilometers from here. My name is Carg and we call our world is *MxDRAA* which as close as you can get is 'Mondara. My people, are Mondaran."

Her expression brightened slightly as she looked at the Captain. "I talked to our medical staff here and they can treat these medical problems you have but you must cross into our world. You need a series of - we call it Quadrazines -to get your neuromuscular imbalance under control. I think that's how you would pronounce it. They said it would take ten of your days."

She put her hand on what was left of Lex's arm, "We've had human guests here for a long time and we know how to use human DNA to regrow most parts of a body. An arm is relatively simple."

Cody seemed particularly awestruck by Carg. She had some sort of allure that Kitty couldn't figure. He took several steps around Carg and almost in a whisper said,

"How beautiful you are."

Kitty thought for sure that she put a spell on poor Cody. He was a goner. How could she do that?

Carg placed her hand on Cody's cheek. "And you are a handsome man, I like that," she said. From then on Cody's eyes had a glazed over look of a puppy about to go on an adventure. Kitty had to give credit to this alter ego of hers, she knew how to dazzle men. She'd probably go after Lex next. Kitty didn't have that ability, she knew that.

Carg continued, "Our engineers must save energy so we only have a short window to use the rift and then it'll close until we can afford to open it again for a return to this world. But there are ten other research groups that want to use the rift. They all want time on it."

She looked at Kitty, "Katherine , I think I know what you will do but you can escape this mad world that's persecuting you or stay here in your own wretched system . I guarantee there's more trouble coming if you stay. I know you."

Kitty knew that Carg was probably right. The reward money would certainly be a help in getting the transponder removed and getting a new identity. Her feel for Ilandia was that you probably could bribe enough people to get them to do anything you wanted. But what good reason could she have for not going over to Carg's side and be free of those worries. Why was she hesitating?

At that moment they heard the air lock open and Sadoka appear,

"The trawler's on AI. If the ride gets bumpy that's not my fault. I want answers ... now! What!" she said in amazement, " There's another person!" She was looking at Carg.

"Where'd she come from and what's the Captain doing   here? He's sick, you know."

"That's why he's here." Kitty said looking at a startled Sadoka. " They can cure him if he goes through the rift ... the worm hole. They're more advanced than we are. They can cure him. And his Laura is on the other side."

Sadoka turned towards Carg and the circle of light. "I've heard of worm holes...I know Captain, you are sick and here there's no chance." She didn't finish and became quiet.

Carg broke the silence, " I have to go back. I have children to take care of and four or five husbands that are...what's your expression... real pains in the ass. That's my world. But we should have enough time to get whoever wants to go to Mondara. You should know that if you wish to return to the system of Sol it may take several of your years before we can do that. It is expensive. But you can return in time."

"We can return?" Lex said with obvious interest.

"Yes, but while you are on our world you may have to be satisfied with some simple pleasures. There are others humans on Mondara that you can associate with, but they never developed a higher culture. All they seem to do is to hunt and fish. Can you imagine. And then they sit around a fire and tell stories. Can you imagine! I think you, Captain, will want to court your Laura again but be warned she will be five years younger than you expect. Those five years in the ice prevented any aging." She hesitated first looking at Lex and then Cody, "And I might have other plans for these gentleman." She turned to Kitty. "You Kitty are my friend and I promise not to insult you any longer. Come to Mondara and be free of these idiots and killers who are persecuting you."

Kitty looked at Carg and narrowed her eyes. "I can guess what you have in mind for Lex and Cody." Kitty looked at her friends who seemed entranced by her and around the Cargo bay and at the boxes of gold and erbium. Yes, the reward money might buy a surgeon, but she had no guarantee of freedom. Only getting Orlando the Rat could finally free her, but she wasn't focused on revenge. It was not fear of the unknown rather it wasn't necessarily love of her world right   here in her familiar solar system, of earth. It was irrational but she had decided.

Kitty looked at Carg with the bright light of the worm hole in back of her. For the Captain it was clear. He wanted to go. To stay behind he would die in a matter of days or weeks, he knew that. If Laura came back to him on this ship she wouldn't have a memory of him and he would still die.

Lex could get his arm back and he needed that to feel whole again. Kitty would have to adjust. Who knows what Carg would do with him. Well, Cody could get into a very interesting situation if he stayed with Carg although she didn't know how he would adjust to Carg's lifestyle, to the lifestyle on Mondara. How many husbands did she say she had? Did she need more. Cody and Lex, Carg's husbands?

She turned to Jason.

"Well Jason, do you have any desire to go to this world of Mondara?" she said.

Jason smiled, "Katherine I would love to see the future and what we might find out in the next thousand years, but I have someone waiting for me."

"Ah, Yes. Darilyn." Carg smiled at that thought. "Good luck to you young man."

Kitty realized she had made up her own mind. "I have decided, Carg, allow the Captain , if he wishes to go through and get quadrazine treatments and meet his Laura. Let Lex through, if he wishes, to get his new arm. Cody if he wishes. I... I will not go through...I'll see what I can do here in the solar system. I will survive."

Carg smiled, "Girl! I guessed you'd do something like this. I won't say it's a dumb choice. No more insults. But I understand. I still have a lot to learn from you and besides my research directors think you are great and have increased the odds on you getting killed in the next year. You stay alive and I will be rich."

The Captain, Cody and Lex made their way to the circle of light then Lex looked back at Katherine, there was a twinkle in his eyes.

"Katherine, I'm glad we met and we did have fun. I want you to know I loved you and every minute of our time together."

Lex lifted the Captain up into the circle of light. Adams could only mumble but they understood him, "Sadoka, you and Jason and Katherine share...the reward." Lex leaned towards Katherine, kissed her on the cheek and said "I love you...come with me."

"Lex, I think I love you too but my life is here. You have a real purpose in going...get a new arm. Then come back."

"Your friend said maybe in a year or two."

"I'll still be here," she said.

Kitty watched as they walked down the tunnel into the world of Mondara. She called after them,

"I'll be waiting for you! Until then." And she stayed there as they walked with Carg leading the way until the worm hole darkened and finally closed. She was alone except for Sadoka by her side and Jason. The three of them were rich- if they could collect the reward.

"All right, Katherine, let's see how you do back with Madam Canzioni. I need a good exciting section for my next installment." Carg's head suddenly rose up in Kitty's imagination, *"I've been telling your story little by little on our world network and the whole nation of Mondara is following what's going on with you."* She now appeared as herself with her dark red hair streaming about, dressed in a deep blue skin tight leotard, since her image was now in Kitty's visual cortex. *"Go to it, Girl!"* She smiled, waved and vanished.

Kitty thought to herself, as best she could. That alter ego will make me famous on that world of hers or I'll be dead. If she can work it, we'll both be rich, but that means staying alive.

164